# The Swordmaster's Secret
# and Other Stories

## The Further Adventures of the Colonial Boy

# Narrelle M Harris

The Swordmaster's Secret and Other Stories © 2024 Narrelle M Harris
Published by Dangerous Charm in 2024
Dangerous Charm
507/225 Elizabeth Street
Melbourne, VIC, 3000
Australia
PRINT ISBN: 978-1-7636499-2-7

The following stories first appeared 2020-2024 at Narrelle M Harris' Patreon at https://www.patreon.com/NarrelleMHarris

- The Swordmaster's Secret
- A Less than Ideal Husband
- God Rest Ye Merry, Gentlemen
- Winter Ice
- The Case of the Vinegar Valentine
- Bored

'The Beekeepers Children' first appeared in Scar Tissue and Other Stories, published by Clan Destine Press in 2019

# Table of Contents

# Foreword

WELCOME TO THIS LITTLE collection of stories set in the universe of *The Adventure of the Colonial Boy (2016)*. In *Colonial Boy*, John Watson is doubly bereaved with the death of his wife Mary and of Sherlock Holmes. Then he receives a telegram from Australia using the old summons from his late friend: 'Come at once if convenient!'

But Sherlock Holmes is dead.

Furious, Watson makes his way to Australia, where he spent some of his boyhood and learned to hide his true nature or pay the price. The journey includes an attempt on his life, and on arrival in Melbourne in 1893 he finds the friend he secretly loved and thought dead is very much alive. They both have a lot to work through if they are going to forgive each other, but first they have to survive the murderous intentions of Moriarty's vengeful lieutenant Sebastian Moran, and a last case together through rural Australia.

Each of these stories takes place after the events of that book, so it's probably fairly obvious that Holmes and Watson work out their troubles and become united once more.

"God Rest Ye Merry, Gentlemen" was written as a kind of Christmas gift for readers; "The Beekeepers Children" was written for inclusion in my collection, *Scar Tissue and Other Stories*, and set in their twilight years in Sussex. Around and between these are the stories written for my Patreon followers.

My heartfelt thanks to these Patrons for their support while the stories were written:

Adelle; D C Sams; Sarah Remy; Julia Hilton; Kim Fasching; Tim Richards; Kimber; Beck; Carey Handfield; sbbeasley; Adam Salisbury;

Alice Harris; Lora Timonin; Melinda McCormack; Milane Duncan-Frantz; Sally; Champagne and Socks; Grant Watson; Jack Fennell; Richard Koehler; Sarah Drosendahl; Tansy Rayner Roberts; and Mike Thompson.

And special thanks to Atlin Merrick for her unstinting support.

I hope you enjoy the further adventures of Sherlock Holmes and his Colonial Boy, Dr John Watson.

Cheers

Narrelle M. Harris

# The Swordmaster's Secret

*'EN GARDE*!' Viscount Douglas Cassell brandished his weapon in a formal salute. In response, Sherlock Holmes mirrored his opponent's stance, holding the wooden rod by its basket hilt. Their singlesticks met between them with a sharp clack. Then they energetically set to: strike and counterstrike, blow and parry, advance and retreat across the floor.

Dr John Watson, watching avidly, leaned against the wall of the Willisden Gentleman's Sword Club gym as he waited for his own sparring partner to appear.

'He's a gifted fighter, your friend.'

John glanced over his shoulder at The Honourable Everett Cassell, who was to train with him today.

'My father is a superb swordsman,' Everett added, 'and yet Mr Holmes keeps pace.'

John was tempted to boast that Sherlock's singlestick skills had saved both their lives in the past, but he held his tongue. During three hard, lonely years of eliminating the last of Moriarty's deadly crew, Sherlock's health had suffered. He had joined the Willisden Gentleman's Sword Club to repair his physique and skills with matches against a talented opponent. John's technique with stick and foil weren't enough of a challenge.

John had also joined the Sword Club to refresh his own rusty swordsmanship, gained with much effort and sweat in the army fifteen years ago. Believing he'd lost Sherlock at Reichenbach, then nearly losing him again last year in Australia, John swore that if an improved sword arm might help to protect his dearest friend, then he'd sweat through the effort again. It didn't hurt that in doing so, he could watch

Sherlock dashing lithely about the gym in his flannel trousers and canvas jacket, as nimble and graceful at forty as he'd been a decade ago.

'Well,' John said to Cassell the Younger, 'I won't be nearly as elegant or proficient as either of them, I'm afraid, but I hope to remember the sword drills, at least.'

'We can start with those to warm up,' offered Everett.

To begin, John balanced his borrowed sabre in his hand, turning it one way and another to test his grip. He'd barely had the opportunity to use a sabre in the field, except for that memorable day at Maiwand. His attention had usually been on treating the wounded – until he became one of their number – but even army doctors learned enough to survive close quarters combat.

John settled into fighting stance. His left hand was behind his back, knuckles resting against his lower spine – a pose which fortunately kept his stiff left shoulder from interfering with his mobility and reach. Most of his weight was back on his sound left leg, which acted as a base and pivot. His scarred right leg took only a fraction of his forward weight, poised to slip back to attention, or to manoeuvre in combat. With this stance, the sabre wasn't a bad weapon for a man of his age and history of injury.

Everett and John moved through the preliminary drills from the *British Infantry Sword Exercise Manual*. Muscle memory was doing wonders for John, though he had already started to perspire when Everett began calling out combinations for attack drills: the Seven Cuts and the parries for those same cuts across the diagonal, vertical and horizontal, ending with sloped swords and a return to attention.

John was breathing more heavily than he'd have liked. Everett had hardly broken a sweat, gliding his way prettily through the moves. The irritating chap was barely in his twenties, thought John, and much more nimble. *But I'm more wily*, he thought, to cheer himself up.

Sherlock and Cassell were still sparring, but as Sherlock deflected another attack, his grey eyes shot John a sultry look. John straightened immediately from his tired slump. Being admired was excellent for one's posture. John had to run his finger underneath his moustache, as though tidying it, to hide his smile.

Cassell's next attack was sudden and from an unexpected angle. Sherlock was slow to parry it and the stick struck his shoulder, hard. Sherlock swiftly counter-attacked, disarming his opponent with a lightning riposte. When he and Cassell shook hands, however, Sherlock winced sharply.

John was immediately at his side. Sherlock demurred, annoyed to have failed to avoid the blow, but when a touch made him hiss, he allowed his doctor to examine the injury.

'No permanent damage, I think,' John concluded. 'Strained, but nothing torn or broken. I can treat this at Baker Street.'

The Viscount apologised sincerely. 'You're so proficient, I wished to push you further. You rallied superbly.'

'Seeking to exceed one's limits is the only way to improve,' Sherlock agreed.

'Best to rest it for today,' said John. He was feeling in need of a rest himself. Young Everett, like his father, had pushed hard.

Later in their rooms, Sherlock's coat, collar and waistcoat were draped over the armchair and the man himself sat on a wooden stool, allowing John to move around him, his hands feeling and testing the shoulder and arm beneath them.

Not entirely satisfied, John scooped an amount of fragrant petroleum jelly from a clay jar into his hands while, on instruction, Sherlock undid the top few buttons of his shirt and pulled his collar to one side. John placed a gentle kiss against Sherlock's temple before he slid a medicinal hand underneath the cloth and began to massage the abused muscles.

'What is this stuff?' Sherlock asked, nose crinkling as he sniffed. 'It's not the usual commercial abomination.'

John, concentrating on his task, didn't reply.

'You don't approve of the ABC Liniment,' Sherlock said.

'No,' John replied. 'It's full of belladonna, aconite and chloroform. It can be dangerous.'

'I hardly think you plan to poison me with it,' Sherlock replied with a smile.

'No, but I also think this is more effective.'

'It smells of fresh cut greenery and faintly of mothballs. The latter is camphor, but I don't recognise the former. Your own patent recipe,' Sherlock concluded.

John smiled. 'Something I learned from the Ayurdevic medicine practitioners in India when I was a boy,' he said. Those long gone days when his father had worked for the East India Company. 'That green smell is the leaves from the nirgundi plant. A little turmeric and a little camphor are blended with the petrolatum too.'

Sherlock closed his eyes and decided to enjoy John's ministrations. His touch had begun to change from the medically professional to a more languorous sensation.

Then they heard a knock on the street-front door, which opened, followed by distinctive heavy footsteps on the stairs.

'Bradstreet,' said Sherlock.

'Yes,' John agreed, having removed his hands from Sherlock. 'I'd recognise that clomping footfall anywhere.' He recapped the clay pot just as there was a rap on the door and Sherlock, affixing his collar, called out curtly, 'Come in, Bradstreet!'

In came the Detective Inspector, bowler hat in hand, grinning broadly. 'You recognise my footsteps, Holmes! I try to vary them, but I never fool you. Oh, but I've interrupted you.'

Sherlock had pulled his waistcoat back on. 'Doctor Watson was seeing to a minor injury I incurred this morning at Willisden's gym.'

'Not bad, I hope?'

'It's nothing to signify,' Sherlock said blithely, before casting a sharp look at their visitor. 'You bring a case?'

'A double murder, I'm afraid,' said Bradstreet, all business again. 'They're clearly linked by the location of their deaths and a social club called the Tybalt, but we can find no reason either man was in Old Deer Park on Sunday night, and the two men died very differently. I hoped you might have some insight for a fresh lead.'

Sherlock was perched in his armchair again, fingers steepled, as though he'd never been half-dressed and receiving medical care when Bradstreet arrived. Bradstreet settled down to share the facts while John took a seat and began to make notes.

'The first body was discovered yesterday morning, Monday, at the Royal Mid-Surrey Golf Club in Richmond,' he said, 'among the trees near the tenth hole.'

'That's a new course,' John supplied to Sherlock. 'Opened while you were... indisposed.'

Sherlock nodded. 'By John Henry Taylor and his friends. The club admits both men and women golfers,' he said, proving that he had been reacquainting himself with the changed particulars of London since his absence. 'Continue, Bradstreet.'

'The dead man was the Honourable Hugh Fernsby, twenty two years of age. He'd been stabbed through the heart with a narrow, long, double-bladed weapon, possibly a rapier, sometime during the night before. The medical examiner believes he would have died almost at once.'

Holmes tapped the tips of his fingers together. 'What else is known about him?'

'Not much. A good lad from a well-respected family. He's the son of Lord Benton Fernsby, who's been so active in the House of Lords of late with the Local Government Act, giving women the right to vote in local elections, among other things.'

Holmes looked as though this was new but uninteresting intelligence. 'A killer would have to be a rare kind of fanatic for that to be a motive.'

'Well, exactly, but none of our inquiries suggest any kind of motive. The young fellow was well liked and had a blameless history, well, apart from a broken engagement. He was to marry Baroness Dacre's daughter last month, but the girl called it off. Lord Benton bought a commission for his son, which the boy was to have taken up next week.'

'What of the other death?'

'Our second victim is Albert Mott,' Bradstreet went on. 'He was found this morning, shot through the heart, tangled in some waterlogged tree roots on the banks of Isleworth Ait, or the tide would have carried the poor beggar away. Another who died instantly. He was a waiter at the Tybalt Club, it seems, though he hadn't been there long.'

'Tell me about this Tybalt club. I have not heard of it.'

'It's simply a new and rather exclusive social club, according to its President, a Mr Alexander Loft. Members meet to discuss theatre, poetry and other literary entertainments, he says. Funny crew. His official title is Prince of Cats, which is from Shakespeare, I know.'

'*Romeo and Juliet*,' murmured John as he wrote this in his book. Sherlock lifted an amused eyebrow at his biographer.

'What is the difficulty?' Sherlock asked, though his eyes were bright. He seemed ready to be off on the scent at once.

'From all accounts, the two dead men barely knew each other. Mott may have served dinners to Fernsby at the club, but they were of very different classes, weren't known to converse, and had no personal ties,' said Bradstreet. 'We explored the evidence to see if they may have killed each other, but that doesn't hold up. No weapons could be found, and since both died instantly, how could one be shot and the other stabbed simultaneously? A third party must have been involved and taken away both weapons, but we have no witnesses to say when Fernsby and Mott entered the grounds, and nothing to indicate where, or whether, a third party was with them. It's early in the investigation, and we're looking into other members of the Tybalt Club, some fifteen in total. They all have alibis, most revolving around them sitting quietly together in their club room on the Strand, reading poetry.' Bradstreet rolled his eyes. 'Some of them are scared, if you ask me, but they're all the sons of the Quality, and we haven't got a skerrick of a clue to pin to anyone. I'm not convinced The Tybalt is a literary club, but what it might be is unclear.'

'What did they say of Mott?'

'He wasn't on shift on Sunday night, and before you ask, Fernsby was meant to be staying with cousins in the country. He never showed. So. Have you anything to suggest?'

'I have several thoughts on the matter,' said Sherlock, 'but I will need to gather more data. Dr Watson, are you free to accompany me today?'

'Wherever you like,' said John, reaching for his coat.

Their first stop was the morgue, where Sherlock examined the bodies of the two men. He paid particular attention to their hands and a small scar on Mott's cheek. Next he looked at their clothing – their shoes and then the tailor's tags of their suits in particular. John peered at their hands as well. He saw calluses and scars that were surprisingly similar on Mott's and Fernsby's right hands.

Sherlock, naturally, told neither Bradstreet nor John a word of his speculations, but his next port of call was the Strand – not the Tybalt club, but in the alley that ran behind the buildings which housed restaurants, theatres, tobacconists and sundry other stores. John kept watch while Sherlock found and questioned a number of men and women taking pre-lunch-rush breaks from their work in that insalubrious location. One man, a waiter of Italian heritage who was lounging against a wall, smoking, nodded at Sherlock. 'Si, si,' he said, followed by a mellifluous torrent of Italian. The gasper between his fingers jabbed perilously close to Sherlock's face as the man gesticulated energetically, but Sherlock never flinched. John wished the fellow would stop waving his hands about.

'Useful?' he asked as they left the alley and made instead for the Tybalt Club entry off the main thoroughfare.

'Indicative,' Sherlock replied. 'It fits with a theory.'

'Which is?'

But the door had opened at their knock, and Sherlock didn't answer as they went inside. They convened at the desk outside the glass door to the Tybalt's library.

Mr Alexander Loft was sardonic and cool and irritated, John saw, the latter not as hidden as the young man intended. The tic of a muscle in his clenched jaw was a tell and the right hand, stuffed into his trouser pocket, was likely clenched.

'We are all truly sorry to hear of Fernsby's death,' said Loft. 'A good fellow. We were all very fond of him.'

'And Mott?'

'Oh, he was a decent enough fellow. Satisfactory in his work, you know. I can't imagine what he was doing out where Fernsby was found.'

'They weren't friends? Or enemies?'

'As I told the fellow from the Yard,' he continued, 'Mott worked here but he had no interactions with poor Fernsby, as far as I knew. Mott was a waiter on busy nights, but mostly he washed dishes.'

'What constitutes a busy night?' Sherlock asked. 'You have a very limited membership, I understand.'

'Small but growing,' said Loft. 'We're a new club.'

'For lovers of literature,' said Sherlock.

'Indeed.' Loft's smile was brittle. 'We have even read the fine works of the good Doctor Watson.' He gave John a sharp smile and John felt unaccountably uncomfortable with the compliment.

'I enjoy the theatre myself,' said Sherlock lightly. 'What are the terms of membership?'

'Oh, we're a tight little circle,' said Loft, just as lightly. 'Membership is by invitation only, I'm afraid. Another member must nominate you.'

'Ah, who are the members then? Perhaps I know-'

'Oh I wouldn't think you'd move in the same circles,' said Loft.

'Oh, but surely that's Victor Burridge, by the window? I know his father well...' and Sherlock, still speaking, pushed open the library door and strode purposefully through the room towards the man in question. John followed on his heels, determined to run interference to allow Sherlock's plan, whatever it was, to come to fruition.

He looked around the clubroom, where several young men were lounging in arm chairs, each with a book held in front of their face in close examination of the text, ignoring Sherlock's intrusion with a ferocity worthy of the Diogenes Club.

'Oh, I beg your pardon,' said Sherlock as the supposed acquaintance scowled at him over the top of his book. 'You're not Victor Burridge.'

'No,' the young man agreed angrily. 'I'm not.'

Sherlock, whom John had never known to be particularly easy to embarrass, shuffled awkwardly, made his apologies, and left with a small nod to the Prince of Cats.

On the Strand, Sherlock was noticeably not at all cowed.

'Did you see their hands?' he asked. 'Their faces?'

'They hid their faces, Sherlock.' Also, John had not been looking at their hands, but he said, 'Were their hands like those of the dead men?'

'To varying degrees, yes. And the club bookshelves were illuminating as well.'

'A pity we'll never be members, then,' said John wryly.

Sherlock gave a bark of laughter. 'Oh, you've read at least one of them before.'

John's response was dry. 'My story collection?'

'At least two, then,' said Sherlock, smile broadening. He hailed a hansom and directed it back to Baker Street.

As the little cab clattered back to Marylebone, John spent a moment gazing at his own hands splayed before him. His thumb and forefinger ached slightly from the sabre grips he'd been practising that morning. He'd remembered to keep his hold in that firm-enough-loose-enough balance that he could adjust, directing the blade as needed. The outside of the knuckle of his forefinger ached slightly from the unaccustomed use, though his left was unblemished.

He frowned. He reached over to take first Sherlock's left hand in his, and then his right, peering closely. He ran his fingers over the mild abrasions on Sherlock's right hand, used so vigorously during the morning's sparring in Willisden.

'Mott had calluses on his right hand,' he said over the sound of hooves and wheels on the cobbles, 'in places that equate with your own hand, and mine. And like ours, his left hand was unmarked.'

Sherlock, content to leave his hand in John's, nodded.

'Fernsby had marks too, though not as significant as Mott's. And... Loft hid his right hand from view, once he knew who you were.'

'He did say he'd read your accounts of my methods.'

'He expected that you would recognise the meaning of any such calluses on his own hand.'

'You're on the trail, John.'

'They were all swordsmen,' John concluded.

'Excellent.'

'But only Fernsby was stabbed,' John mused. 'The waiter was shot.'

'I doubt waiting tables was his trade,' said Sherlock. 'The Italian in the alley told me that Mott and the other staff from that club were all French and generally bad at their jobs. Mott's clothes carried French labels. And he had the hands of a swordsman too, remember.'

'And their shoes?'

'Comfortable, slightly worn in patterns that suggest fencing. Despite being partially immersed in the river water, Mott's shoes and socks as well as Fernsby's held traces of clipped grass of the type found on a golfing green. They were definitely together at the site where Fernsby died.'

John finally released Sherlock's hand as the cab clipped along Oxford Street. 'Both swordsmen. A death by sword but another man shot. No motive.'

'Don't forget the Prince of Cats, John.'

'Tybalt. *Romeo and Juliet.* I don't see how that explains anything.'

'It doesn't, yet, but it's suggestive. I have ideas but the linchpin that links them eludes me. I need to review the papers of the week, and then consult an expert, and things should be clearer.'

Back in Baker Street, Sherlock wasted no time in reducing their sitting room to wild disarray, hunting through the numerous papers of the week. John stood in the middle of the storm, with a newspaper in each hand and a baffled expression.

'What am I looking for?'

'Gossip and society news, John. Fernsby, probably, or perhaps Loft. The other chap I contrived to get a look at was Reginald Davenport, son of Lord Horace Davenport. He has the same calluses on his right hand, and he wore an Eton tie. I suspect one has to be from a particular graduate group of Old Etonians for an invitation to the Tybalt.'

John was rummaging through newspapers and throwing them aside with as much vigour as Sherlock.

'So they schooled together. Ran a fencing club, perhaps?'

'At school, yes. I think they've advanced from fencing. Aha!' Sherlock waved a newspaper in triumph and brought it over. John examined the entry, which presented a sombre account of Hugh Fernsby, Reginald Davenport, Alexander Loft and several other young men attending the funeral of their late friend, Edward Charles Perrault, a fellow Etonian. 'It says he died in a presumed hunting accident on his family's estate,' Sherlock said meaningfully.

'Inferring murder?'

'Or suicide.'

'Surely this only makes the case more opaque.'

'No, no, my dear fellow. The picture is not yet clear, but we have more details. I am going out to seek further clarification and to send some telegrams. Stay here to receive them, and I'll return in an hour or so.'

'I'd rather-'

'I know. But you're better use to me here.' Sherlock pressed a hurried kiss to John's lips, which sealed the doctor's obedience, and dashed back downstairs to Baker Street.

When Sherlock returned, John had four telegrams open on the dining table, pressed flat and held down with salt and pepper shakers and two chess pieces. Langdale Pike's name was attached to two of the messages, DI Bradstreet to the third, and the fourth hailed from France.

Pike's first message read: PERRAULT AND FERNSBY SAID TO BE CLOSER THAN BROTHERS.

His second read: ELIZABETH DACRE REPORTEDLY SAID THAT SHE WOULD FORGIVE FERNSBY IF HE WOULD FORGIVE HIMSELF.

Bradstreet's telegram read: FERNSBY ALIBI LATE TO VISITING PERRAULT ESTATE. FOUL PLAY UNPROVEN. SUSPECTED SELF MURDER.

The French telegram read: LA MOTTE WANTED IN RELATION TO INCIDENT IN MONTPARNASSE.

Sherlock perused them with satisfaction. 'This fits with what I learned from Baroness Dacre, who told me almost nothing so loudly that the facts were unmistakable.'

Intrigued, John gestured for Sherlock to continue.

'I'll explain on the way,' Sherlock said. 'I have a few technical questions to ask of Viscount Cassell about duelling and its traditional rules, to be sure of the events.'

So off they went to Willisden in another hansom.

'Duelling is illegal,' said John grimly as they set out, 'and has been for 75 years.'

'Yet in France the practice continues, within strictly defined rules of combat, and it continues here despite the law.'

'You think this Perrault fellow was killed in a duel?'

'Yes, though I think his death was not intended. I believe Hugh Fernsby made some fatal error and killed his friend, an act witnessed by other members of this Tybalt club.'

'Clearly not a literary club.'

'No.' Sherlock smiled thinly. 'The book I noted on their shelves was the *British Infantry Sword Exercise Manual*, sitting in the midst old treatises by Henry Angelo Senior and his son, as well as recent books by Egerton Castle and Alfred Hutton. You may be aware they have been reviving the techniques of the old fencing masters.'

'But why would Fernsby be duelling with his friend? What quarrel could they have had?'

'There we come to supposition,' Sherlock confessed, 'but Pike's telegrams and Baroness Dacre's clear fury, and even disgust, suggest a confrontation with a spurned lover.'

John blinked in confusion, and then his gaze darkened to sorrow. 'Perrault and Fernsby closer than brothers, Pike said. And Fernsby was to marry. Oh.'

'Yes,' agreed Sherlock solemnly. 'Fernsby was about to abandon Perrault for a wife. Perhaps in a fit of despair, he demanded a duel. They were members of a duelling club, after all.'

John had winced at the mention of a lover abandoned for a wife. Sherlock took a moment to close a hand over John's in the privacy of the cab. 'It is no reflection on you, John, or your choices. Or mine, come to that. We each did what we must, guided by what we felt it best to do at the time, within our experiences and the limitations available to us. Now we have new experience, and new choices.'

John turned his hand up so that they clasped hands, palm to palm. 'We at least have lived long enough to learn from our regrets. I grieve for them, Sherlock. If what you say is true, Perrault confronted the man he loved and was losing, and Fernsby faced him, torn by their own limitations and choices. And one of them died. But, then, what happened to Fernsby on Sunday night? That fatal wound could not have been self-administered. Someone killed him. And that French swordsman, Mott, pretending to be a waiter – what was he doing there?'

'La Motte, his real name as you saw by the telegram from the Sûreté, has been involved in duelling before. I believe he may have been brought over to train the duelling club and acted as a second at the golf club for what was surely a retaliatory duel due to Perrault's death. Perrault was a fellow Etonian in that little group of friends, and must have been a member.'

They unclasped their hands as the hansom swept into the street leading to the Willisden Gentleman's Sword Club.

'You think Viscount Cassell can help in some way?' John prompted.

'I wish a word with the Viscount on who in London might have the skills to be the other parties – the swordsman and his second – in this duel. A man of his talent must be aware of London's most promising fencers, especially those from the finest schools.'

'Might they be another member of the Tybalt Club?'

'I'm sure of it,' said Sherlock. 'Some may view it as a rebellious hobby, mere dilettantes, but they are named for an infamous and aggressive duellist, after all. '

'Tybalt killed Mercutio,' said John.

'Just so.'

'And then Romeo killed Tybalt.'

'Yes.'

John shook his head at the waste of it all.

Viscount Douglas Cassell did not seem pleased to see them, though he was civil enough as he asked, 'You've returned for more training already?'

'I've come to consult you on a case,' said Sherlock, unconcerned, though John knew that he was aware of the swordmaster's suppressed displeasure.

'If it is in my power to assist, I shall,' said Cassell.

As Sherlock outlined the nature of his request, his son Everett emerged from the gymnasium's changing rooms. His pale skin was flushed with anxiety, his motions agitated.

'You're back,' he said flatly.

'Holmes is pursuing a case,' John explained. 'He consults other experts from time to time, and is hoping the Viscount can help to identify a killer.'

The pronouncement startled Everett. 'What would my father know of such things?'

'We're seeking a young swordsman. He may have gone to Eton,' said John. 'Actually, you might know of someone who fits the bill.'

'Me? No. Nobody. I...'

Behind them came and angry cry and John turned sharply around to see the Viscount bearing a rapier and advancing, slashing, on Sherlock. Sherlock darted beyond his reach, but a wall was behind him, shutting off escape.

John began to run towards him, only to find Everett Cassell cutting him off.

'Father said Holmes was dangerous,' snarled Everett. He held a sabre in each hand. John stopped, poised and ready for a fight, knowing he couldn't last long without a weapon. If he could at least get between Sherlock at the Viscount...

'Here,' snarled Everett, and he tossed one of the sabre towards John. 'Never let it be said I did not obey the rules. I am a gentleman.'

John caught the weapon by the hilt and deftly wrapped his fist around it, and with no further warning, Everett attacked.

The morning's drills had awoken his long-ago training, and despite Everett's youth and vigour, John managed to parry and evade. He attacked too, and forced the boy back, but then would be on the defensive again.

Everett was not holding back. He meant his strikes to be killing blows. John had seen that murderous light in eyes before: at Maiwand, and with Sherlock in London and across England when miscreants saw the inevitable end was near.

Knowing that one slip might mean death, John tried not to be distracted by the sight of Sherlock in the corner of his eye – weaponless but not defenceless.

Sherlock had drawn his fob watch and chain from his waistcoat pocket and, with the watch as anchor, whipped the long chain at the Viscount's eyes, striking a small, stinging blow. In that moment, Sherlock pulled a kerchief from his pocket and flung that, too, at his opponent's face, obscuring Cassell's aim once more. This defence was among the deep principles of bartitsu – to use whatever tools came to hand against your attacker.

While the Viscount was slicing the cloth out of his line of sight, Sherlock turned and kicked, a sharp and savage jujitsu strike to Cassell's thigh, then another.

John sensed Everett's next move and refocused. Everett struck a jarring blow which John only parried just in time, and John's memory was flooded with those awful minutes on the field of Maiwand, fighting for his life before a bullet in his shoulder, another in his thigh, took him down. His mind's eye was flooded, too, with the image of Sherlock fighting now for his life, too, *sans* sword or pistol.

Everett sliced a cut towards him and John's adrenalin-fuelled army training surged to the fore.

Everett Cassell was a gentleman, and fought like one. But John Hamish Watson, while gentlemanly enough, was a doctor and a soldier, and he knew the battlefield was full of dirty fighting – full of the imperative to wound or kill your opponent as quickly as possible, so that you might yourself survive.

So as Everett Cassell's sabre blade cut down, John's own blade came up to parry and knock Cassell's arm wide. Then he reached across with his left hand to hold Everett's right wrist in a steel grip, and, fist around the hilt of his sword, John punched Everett directly in the face with the basket of the sabre.

Everett, nose broken, face scraped by the metal, blinded with blood, shouted in surprised pain. John kicked him hard in the crotch and, when the screaming boy was down, he stamped hard on the wrist that held the sword and heard a crunch.

He kicked Everett's blade clear of the melee and whirled to go to Sherlock's aid.

In the few seconds disarming Everett had taken, Sherlock had retrieved a long fighting stick that had been mounted on the wall and, combined with his startling bartitsu fighting techniques, unfamiliar to the Viscount, was keeping beyond Cassell's blade. But John could see that Sherlock's morning injury was affecting the movement of his shoulder. Cassell's rapier descended swiftly on the stick, cracking it in two. Sherlock was forced back against the table holding a dry water basin and a small stack of towels.

With a roar, John ran at Viscount Cassell, sabre at the ready. The rapier, he knew, would have longer reach, but the important thing was to distract him, to allow Sherlock time to escape.

Cassell whipped the rapier up, and John could see how it would get under his guard if he continued forward, so he made a single turn as he ran – the rapier missed his waist by inches – and then, facing front again, too close now to use the blade, he grabbed for Cassell's extended sword arm, tried to hold it, slipped...

But there was Sherlock with a towel in his right hand. Holding one end tight, he flicked the other towards the left of Cassell's neck, close enough to press his forearm against Cassell's throat; the cloth flew across and around the back of Cassell's neck. Sherlock reached for the other end of it as it slapped against Cassell's Adam's apple, seized it, pulled it tight, right forearm now pressed across his opponent's windpipe, the cloth compressing his carotid artery.

John seized Cassell's sword arm again and relieved him of the rapier as he fell swiftly though briefly unconscious.

Sherlock and John stood, panting, over the man as he began to stir again and, across the gymnasium, his son moaned and nursed his broken wrist.

'You're unharmed?' John demanded.

'I'm embarrassed,' Sherlock muttered. 'I wasn't expecting this.' Then he looked into John's eyes, his own full of concern. 'And you?'

John grinned, a rather savage expression on his red and sweating face. 'Never better.'

'Best restrain this one, then, while I send for Bradstreet.'

John saluted him with his sabre, then set it aside so he could tie the Viscount's wrists with a torn towel, before he went to provide first aid to the not so Honourable Everett Cassell.

The boy was crying.

'It was only ever meant to be fun. A lark. Fencing was so dull but duelling was exciting. I swear to you, nobody was supposed to die, but then Neddy Perrault lost his head and challenged Fernsby, and poor Fernsby was in such a lather that Perrault would expose their relations before the wedding that he took him up, pistols at dawn, and the next thing, Perrault's blood was everywhere and Hugh Fernsby was a killer!'

Sherlock returned, having sent a street lad to find a bobby. 'You're a member of the Tybalt Club. You went to school with Loft, Fernsby and the others.'

Everett nodded miserably.

'What happened at the golf club on Sunday?'

'Loft said the duelling rules meant we had to challenge Fernsby, to make things right, since Fernsby was getting ready to fess up to what happened to Neddy. That would have got all of us in trouble. I told my father what was going on and he arranged for me to challenge Hugh, only Hugh came with a second, the La Motte fellow, and said he wanted to negotiate satisfaction. He said he'd keep quiet after all. He would take up his commission and leave England, whatever Liz, his fiancée, said.' He glanced fearfully across the room at his father, who had deflated terribly, his face ashen.

'I killed Hugh Fernsby,' said the Viscount quietly but firmly. 'And I pursued and shot the witness, that Frenchman, to protect my boy. Everett was foolish but he's not a killer.'

Everett Cassell had been in a killing mood a short while ago, John knew, but he was suddenly exhausted. That boyish folly, fed by the entitlement of wealth and position, had come to this was sickening. Bradstreet and the courts could sort it out.

If Sherlock had other ideas, he shared them only in a low-spoken exchange with DI Bradstreet and his men when they arrived, after a sidelong look at John sagging on a stool, exhausted, eyes haunted.

Mrs Hudson brought up hot water to fill two basins and clean towels, and left before John had to pretend to carry his jug upstairs to his room. Instead, he and Sherlock both repaired to Sherlock's room to bathe.

John ached all over. Sherlock was more spritely, but the arm he'd injured in the morning was mottled with bruises.

'I think Cassell thought we were already on his trail this morning,' said Sherlock ruefully as he ran a sponge over his body. 'When we returned, he was sure of it. My deepest apologises, John. I missed the link between his son and the boys from Eton. He wasn't named in the funeral article, and I wasn't aware. I put you in the gravest danger.'

John, who had already washed and was sitting on the edge of Sherlock's bed in a clean nightshirt, shook his head. 'I'm a tough old bird. Almost as hard to kill as you are, and many have tried.'

Sherlock threw the sponge back into the basin and turned with a scowl.

'Don't.'

John sighed, acknowledging the many meanings in the word. *Don't make light of it. Don't be cavalier with your life. Don't die.*

Sherlock took a calming breath, then pressed a kiss to the top of John's head. 'We shall have to be more careful. I will not lose you now.'

John tilted his head up. 'No. Nor I you.'

Sherlock's fingers brushed John's cheek. 'You were thinking of Maiwand today.'

'Yes. It reminded me how to fight.'

'Good.'

They kissed then, mouths gentle on each other.

'John,' murmured Sherlock, willingly letting John draw him down into an embrace.

'Mmm?' John rested his cheek against Sherlock's collar bone and closed his eyes, contented, the old stresses and fears melting out of his body in the comfort of this intimacy.

'Where's the liniment?'

'My bag,' John murmured. He was beginning to drift into sleep. He mumbled a protest as Sherlock disentangled himself, then hummed in sleepy pleasure when Sherlock helped him to remove the shirt and began to apply the pleasant-smelling mixture to John's aching muscles.

'I sometimes make the mistake of underestimating you, John,' he said, hands rubbing down John's biceps and up over the scar of the old shoulder wound.

'Don't do that,' slurred John in an amused tone. 'Leave that to the enemy.'

He didn't see the smile that elicited from Sherlock. 'All right,' Sherlock agreed. 'If you write any more stories, keep hiding your light under a bushel, then. You will be my secret weapon.'

John's moustache shifted with his contented smile, but any reply was lost as he fell into contented sleep.

# A Less than Ideal Husband

IN DECEMBER OF 1894, Sherlock Holmes was melodramatically lamenting the last crisp, cold days of autumn as devoid of interest or any redeeming feature. 'The criminals of London cannot stir themselves to action, John,' he muttered darkly, peering out the bay window at a street innocent of mayhem. The late sunrise barely illuminated the view. 'They lack ambition, imagination and courage.'

Dr John Watson only smiled faintly from his armchair by the fire, where he had been scouring the early edition papers for potential cases. He was used to this litany. His Holmes hated to be bored.

'You've only yourself to blame, you know,' John said fondly. 'They got used to you being dead over the last few years, and now you're back and in the papers and they're very aware that you'll ruin Christmas for them, given half a chance.'

Sherlock had barely bothered to dress today, opting to pull his dressing gown over trousers and shirt, and forgoing a collar altogether while he shoved his feet into slippers. He flopped into his chair and regarded his doctor ruefully across the carpet. 'Word has travelled quickly. And you've not even resumed writing about our cases for *The Strand*, though I see *The Illustrated Police News* has taken up doing so, with even more sensationalism and less accuracy.'

'You won't get a rise out of me with that any more, Sherlock,' said John, turning a page nonchalantly. 'You only turn literary critic when you want me flustered, and you've much more interesting ways of flustering me now.' He regarded Sherlock over the top of his paper, brown eyes sparkling with invitation. 'It's early in the day, but I'm perfectly prepared to be flustered to help you tackle boredom.'

Sherlock was the one flustered now. They had been back in London almost eleven months; they had been lovers a few months longer than that, after their difficult reunion in Australia last year. He should be used to this intimacy now, and the easy way John alluded to it, and invited it, and acted on it. Theirs had been a history of denial, however, and Sherlock still found their new status a continuing surprise. Always welcome, of course, and always accompanied by the knowledge of what it would cost them both if they were discovered.

But they were clever men, and safe in their own home, and discovery here was unlikely.

Sherlock rose, plucked the newspaper from John's fingers and, after flicking the tails of his dressing gown out of the way, sat on John's lap, knees either side of his hips.

'I require your urgent attention,' he announced in a quiet, commanding tone.

'You have it,' laughed John, and they kissed.

Several minutes later, the ring of the bell downstairs alerted them to the mid-morning arrival of a client, resulting in the abrupt termination of their intimacies.

Sherlock sprang to his feet. John snatched up the paper with one hand while smoothing down his ruffled moustache and then his hair with the other. Sherlock retreated into the bedroom to correct his more advanced state of deshabille.

The parlour door opened a minute later. 'Mr Morell, for Mr Holmes,' announced Mrs Hudson, taking the man's hat, gloves and cane. She withdrew after a meaningful look to John's collar. His hand flew up to adjust a button as he rose.

'Won't you take a seat, Mr Morell? Mr Holmes will be with us in a moment, I'm sure.'

The far door opened on cue and through it came Holmes, still in his mouse-brown dressing gown over re-buttoned and presentable trousers and shirt, but now properly shod and with his collar attached.

His hair was neatly combed. His cheeks were flushed still, though he'd obviously decided this was a feature to emphasise rather than hide.

'Forgive my appearance,' said Sherlock grandly as he swept energetically into the parlour, 'I have just returned from an invigorating case at the docks. A curious affair pertaining to the steamboat *Matilda Briggs*. It's almost a shame Dr Watson has abandoned his habit of jotting down his capricious accounts of our cases, although the giant rat of Sumatra is perhaps beyond a curious public's willingness to accept as fact.' Sherlock's dancing grey eyes skittered over John's, noting that the doctor was trying not to laugh at these outrageous lies.

'Mr Holmes,' interrupted the tall man on their rug, 'If I have come at an inconvenient hour, I'll return at another. I'm a very busy man, however, and I'd be glad of five minutes of your time.'

'Ah! I see that our visitor is a man of the theatre.' Sherlock addressed himself to Mr Morell. 'Please take a seat. Note, Watson, there is a determination about the jaw yet a sensitivity about the lips and eyes which denotes an artist of some description. But the lack of calluses on the hands or the tell-tale lines of a squint show he works not in paint or stone but in human clay. See how naturally he commands the little stage of Baker Street's living room; his clear diction and ringing voice.'

Mr Morell seated himself with an air of bonhomie, taking these observations as compliments.

'Indeed, Mr Holmes. I am HH Morell, actor and co-manager of the Haymarket Theatre, and I hope you may be able to help me in a delicate matter.' He cast a doubtful eye towards Watson.

'Dr Watson's discretion can be relied upon as readily as my own,' Holmes told him firmly. 'Please tell us what afflicts your current production. Mr Wilde's latest, isn't it?'

'Yes – *An Ideal Husband*. We're in rehearsals this month for a January opening, after some delay,' said Morell.

'Of what nature?' asked Sherlock.

'John Hare commissioned the play originally in 1893, but didn't like the ending. Then Lewis Waller, one of the Haymarket's principals and my co-manager, took it on after the senior manager, Mr Tree, went to America. Waller is playing Sir Robert Chilte–'

'Mr Morell, does the play's late production impinge on the matter at hand?'

Morell cleared his throat. 'I believe it's unrelated. The current issue is some funny business with a prop.'

Sherlock steepled his fingers together in an attitude of attention while Dr Watson took up his notebook and pencil to capture the salient details.

'The play requires a particular item,' said Mr Morell, 'a diamond brooch, used in the first three Acts. It's missing.'

'Your props master can acquire another, surely?'

Morell's hands clenched then unclenched. 'Easily enough. However, another brooch was on the floor beside the properties shelf this morning.'

'So a substitute has been found?'

'It's not really suitable. Not big enough to be seen by the farther seats. The problem is,' he added before Sherlock could express impatience, 'the one we found is made of real diamonds, real silver, real rubies, as well. It is of *real* value. Nobody knows how it came into the theatre, who left it behind, or who owns it. It may be a practical joke; it may be something stranger or malicious, but of course, such a valuable piece will be *missed* by someone.'

'Let me see,' said Sherlock, and held out his hand imperiously. Morell dipped two fingers into his waistcoat pocket and drew out a slender brooch in the shape of a Scottish thistle. A ruby made up the bulb of the flower, with diamonds marking out the tuft atop the bulb, and small diamond chips shone in elegant lines down the body of leaves and stem. A simple but sturdy clasp showed it had not broken and then fallen from a dress or cloak. It might have slipped open and come free or been deliberately removed.

'You don't think it's an innocent mistake?' John asked.

'What possible mistake would account for the loss of a paste brooch and the appearance of this handsome thing? They don't even look alike: the brooch is round and bulky and the thistle is elegant and slender; completely inappropriate for the brooch's role on the stage.'

Sherlock spent several minutes studying the narrow brooch before tossing it to John, who caught it neatly and held it up to the light.

'It's beautiful,' said John. 'The diamonds glitter even in this low light, and the ruby is a gorgeous deep red. The workmanship on the silver is intricate, too. It must have cost a pretty sum.'

'It must,' agreed Morell, 'and I won't have someone causing trouble at my theatre by either being a thief, or accusing my people of theft. I want to find out where it came from, and send it back with all speed!'

'Well,' said Sherlock, rising. 'Let us go to the theatre, Doctor Watson, and unravel this little mystery.'

The Haymarket looked grand enough from Suffolk Street, with its high-pillared entrance. Inside, though, the magic wrought by night was rendered prosaic by day. The painted wood, aged curtains and worn furnishings of the theatre and its stalls – which pretended to finer things by limelight, costume and ringing speeches – were tawdry in the dim light, shown up for make-believe.

Morell led the detective and his friend down the central aisle to the foot of the stage. A few shadows were moving in the wings and backstage.

'The cast aren't here?' John asked.

'Rehearsals won't start until well after lunch,' said Morell. 'However, we have the staff and backstage crew making things ready and checking the lights.'

A short, neat red-headed man with a trimmed ginger beard and an air of brisk competence detached from the rear shadows and walked downstage.

'Mr Morell, sir,' he said, 'I've fetched an identical brooch from the same feller at the market. A hundred identical gewgaws there if this 'n goes missing as well. It only cost a few pence. I've put the receipt and change into petty cash. Did you find who owns the thistle pin?'

'Not yet, Aubrey, but I've asked these gentlemen to assist. Mr Holmes, Dr Watson, this is Aubrey Teller, our stage manager.'

Sherlock regarded the man keenly. 'Mr Teller. Can you show me where the missing brooch was stored, and the other found?'

Teller led the men across the stage and into the wings, where a set of shelves sat ready with the items required for the play. A clearly drawn note in chalk showed an Act for each shelf, and divided the shelves into sections for each item, character and performer who required the item. A square labelled Act 1 was marked 'diamond brooch/Mrs Cheveley/ Miss F West' and the new brooch sat in the centre of the space. Similar but empty spaces for the piece appeared on shelves labelled for the remaining Acts.

'The stage brooch should have been here. I found the other on the floor behind the shelves when I was looking for ours.'

'I take it,' said Sherlock, 'that at the end of each Act, the brooch would be moved to its next empty space on the shelf, ready for its next appearance.'

'Just so, Mr Holmes,' said Teller. 'It doesn't get used again after the end of Act Three, so I retrieve it then from Miss Florence West and return it to the Act One position. All nice and orderly.'

'And you retrieved it from Miss West as usual at the end of rehearsals yesterday?'

'Indeed. It was right here on the Act One shelf when I locked up last night, and gone this morning. Hoskins can confirm, as he was the one who reported the loss to me. Hoskins!'

A thin man with dark, curly hair and a good deal of chalk dust on his hands, trousers and waistcoat bobbed up from the other side of the stage. His hair was patchwork white with the stuff. 'Sir?'

Teller raked the man with a gaze and lifted an eyebrow. 'Are you exploring costume ideas for a Christmas ghost story on the Haymarket's time, Mr Hoskins?'

Hoskins tried to rub chalk dust out of his hair, only to add more to the ghostly effect. 'Still cleaning up the chalk box that got dropped off the shelves and danced on, it looked like. Picked it up and the bottom fell out of it. Chalk everywhere,' he grumbled. 'Made a right mess. Might need a bit more from petty cash to replace the chalk.'

'Later is soon enough. This is Mr Holmes.'

Hoskins looked delighted underneath all the chalk, which had now spread to his forehead and nose. '*The* Mr Holmes? Mr *Sherlock* Holmes? It's an honour! It's been delightful to read you're back in London, sir, and not half as dead as reported.'

John preened on Sherlock's behalf, while Sherlock covered his sudden and unexpected emotion at the welcome with a brisk nod and a focus on the business at hand. 'Very kind. Now, can you tell me what else was amiss with your props shelf this morning?'

'Apart from my crushed box of chalk and the space where the Cheveley brooch should have been? Nothing at all. Everything else was present and correct.'

'Nice and orderly, in fact?'

'Well, not as orderly as it ought to have been. I like to place things just so at the end of the night. Neat, you see. Easy to see at a glance what's what. This morning it was off-kilter. Not a shambles, just not right. The spoon here was on top of the fake letter instead of to one side, and the saucers that go with the tea set were at the front instead of the back. One dish had a slight crack but nothing was broken or missing. Oh, and Lord Chiltern's cigarette case and lighter were side by side instead of the lighter on top. I was very annoyed.' And he sounded it.

Sherlock, on the other hand, began to examine thoroughly the props shelves, scanning quickly at first, then dropping to his hands and knees, nose pressed almost to the floorboards. He whipped his magnifying glass from his pocket and peered more closely still at the cracks between the boards and then almost crawled across them, following a path that led behind the curtains. He lifted aside a length of heavy cloth, gave a loud Ha! of satisfaction and returned to the props shelf, where he held out his hand. John stepped up and placed a pair of tweezers and an envelope in Sherlock's waiting fingers. A moment later, Sherlock had picked up several small items from the cracks, dropped them into the envelope, and rose.

'Who closed up the theatre after rehearsals?' he asked.

'After the cast and crew and Mr Morell left,' said Teller, 'I did.'

'And everyone had gone home?'

'They'd left, at any rate. Home for some. The club or a public house for supper and champagne, otherwise.'

'Naturally. Did any of them return during the night?'

'Nobody. Well, except for Mr Wilde. He said he'd left his cane in the stalls, though I hadn't seen it when I did my rounds before locking up. Mr Wilde had his own key, though, and he said he'd lock up once he found it.'

'And the thistle pin isn't his?'

'I never saw him wear it, Mr Holmes,' said Teller. Morell and Hoskins agreed, when asked, that it was an unlikely piece for the playwright to wear.

'It's a costly bit of sparkle, suited to Mr Wilde's purse,' said Teller, 'but not to his style. Wrong country, you see. He's a dandy, all right, but if Mr Oscar Wilde wore a gem it'd be an emerald for Ireland, not a Scotch thistle.'

'But some of his friends might wear it?' suggested John suddenly.

'Ladies and gentlemen of his acquaintance might,' Teller agreed. 'I swear I haven't seen it before, though and his friends haven't been here for rehearsals.'

'I'd like to take a look at this chalk box of yours,' Sherlock said.

Puzzled, Hoskins led the way to the opposite wing, and a bucket full of broken chalk and rags infused with the chalk dust he'd been clearing away. Sherlock examined the mangled cardboard box then dropped it into the bucket again. He took out a cloth to wipe his fingers.

'When is Mr Wilde returning to the theatre?'

'He is due early this evening, when rehearsals are underway again,' said Morell. 'But I sent a messenger to him. He states the brooch isn't his.'

'Ah well. I'm sure he knows best. Nevertheless. Would you permit that I take possession of the thing. I believe I know who its rightful owner is, and how it came to be here. It might be best all round if I returned it myself and leave the theatre out of it.'

Mr Morell gazed at Sherlock, dumbfounded. 'But who? And how?'

'A late visitor,' said Sherlock, 'who bumped against your props shelf. As well as displacing some items and cracked the saucer, he knocked over and stood on the chalk box and the glass brooch, crushing both. I found glass and chalk dust between the boards, but the clean-up was hasty and incomplete, leaving your Mr Hoskins to the more arduous task of the chalk dust.'

'And the brooch...'

'Became unhooked and fell. Nothing more sinister, but I think both Mr Wilde and the visitor would prefer our discretion.'

A brief but meaningful silence fell. Mr Morell and his staff were fully aware of the types of late night visitor a man might bring to an empty theatre where jewellery might come adrift and cupboards knocked, and wish to keep that visit a secret from his wife.

'Take the thing, then,' said Morell, handing it over, 'and if anyone comes looking for it I will refer them to you.'

'Yes, that would be the best course.'

Sherlock placed the expensive thistle brooch into his coat pocket and strode out of the theatre. John said goodbyes for them both and followed on his heels.

'Do you know who the lady is, Sherlock?' he asked.

'This belongs to no lady,' Sherlock said.

'I was being polite, Sherlock. We don't know if she's his mistress.'

'Mr Wilde does not have a mistress.'

'Then...?'

Sherlock stopped and turned to give John an exasperated glare. 'Do you really pay no attention to rumours?'

'Not in broad daylight on the streets of London, I don't,' said John, very quietly.

Sherlock's expression softened. 'That is because you are a gentleman,' he said. 'All right. I believe we will find Mr Wilde at his London residence at this hour, possibly still abed. And since I don't know where to find his friend, the owner of the pin, we will visit Mr Wilde.'


If John thought Sherlock's morning habits were lax, he at least found them appealing. He liked that he was the only one who ever saw Sherlock in nightshirt and bare feet, hair flopped over one eye and movement languid with contented lassitude.

Mr Oscar Wilde was nominally dressed and in a dressing gown, not unlike Sherlock had been that morning, but to John it felt more of a performance piece. As though the man famous for his quips and wittily defying society had taken clothes *off* and disarranged the rest in order to make a louche impression on his guests.

John was not entirely sure he liked Mr Wilde, or his works. The fairy tales and ghost stories were diverting enough, and the plays astute, but that *Dorian Gray* of his was so archly and self-consciously witty –hardly two pages could pass without some hollow, meaningless epithet designed to show off the author's cleverness – that it was hard to enjoy. At least when Sherlock was showing off, it was generally to the detriment of scoundrels and the benefit of society.

Well, John had to acknowledge, sometimes it was Sherlock's way of flirting, too, and on the whole, John decided at that moment, he'd stop comparing the two because maybe they had more in common than brilliant minds and a penchant for dressing gowns.

Mr Wilde had draped himself on a sofa and regarded them with drooping eyelids and a secret smile, visible through the smoke of the cigarette he held in his fingers.

'Oh yes, I did go back to the theatre last night,' he said lazily, answering Sherlock's question. 'I was only there a moment. Retrieving my cane.' His eyes flicked towards a handsome and whimsical parade cane of blue-green glass. John found it unlikely that the efficient Mr Teller would have missed it on his rounds.

Sherlock didn't bother to refute the playwright's claim. He only took the thistle pin from his pocket and held it up to the light. The diamonds sparkled. The ruby glowed a rich red.

'This lapel pin belongs to your friend, Lord Alfred Douglas. He wears the thistle in honour of his family title, the Marquess of Queensberry, which is in the Peerage of Scotland.'

Wilde gazed at the pin with a rueful expression. 'So he does.'

'You were no doubt showing him around the set.' Sherlock's tone suggested that this was a euphemism.

Wilde's expression sharpened at the tone. He studied Sherlock, head to toe, and suddenly he relaxed. He made a show of rising, walking to Sherlock and taking the pin from Sherlock's hand, ensuring that their fingers brushed in the taking.

'No doubt, Mr Holmes.' He smiled winsomely. 'I could show *you* around the set some evening, if you like.' Sherlock's face remained immobile. Oscar Wilde then bent his light blue eyes and all of his charisma, upon John Watson. 'Or your handsome friend.'

John fussed with his moustache, awkward at the compliment.

'A fine moustache, Dr Watson,' noted Mr Wilde, making John even more discomfited. 'Though, to reach the Hellenic ideal of manliness, you should be clean-shaven.'

John blinked; his eyes went wide and his ears went pink, but he said, 'I wasn't aware that my manliness was in question.'

'Oh, not at all, my good doctor. Far from it.' Wilde's expression was somehow both wilfully innocent and the exact opposite.

Sherlock's mouth was pressed in a thin, disapproving line. 'I trust you will return that pin to Lord Alfred,' he said primly, 'before questions are asked about its disappearance.'

Wilde pinned the item to his dressing gown. 'I will return it to Bosie this afternoon, without fail.'

'And perhaps more discretion when showing him or any of your other friends around the theatre might prevent other losses which would unfairly implicate the good people of that theatre.'

'Ah,' said Wilde, arms lifting in a very actorly pose. 'It is absurd to divide people into good and bad. People are either charming or tedious.'

'Which was your Dorian Gray meant to be?' asked Sherlock, in a tone of light disinterest. 'I forget.'

'I don't believe that for a moment,' Wilde replied. 'I have read all of your exploits, Mr Holmes, and the whole meaning of your life is to remember all and to know all so that you may judge all.'

'I observe all,' Sherlock conceded stiffly. 'My judgement is my own, and I act accordingly.'

'As do we all, Mr Holmes.' Wilde's smile had become thinner.

'Including your wife, I'm sure,' said Sherlock acidly.

Wilde became very still, his face very pale then red with anger. But his next words did not touch on his personal life at all.

'Congratulations, by the way, on becoming a modern Lazarus, though considerably later than four days after your death,' he said cheerfully. 'Was it Doctor Watson who performed that miracle for you? Was he sent a message that 'He whom you love is ill', as it says in John 11?'

Sherlock's face went even paler than Wilde's. John, already regretting the turn of the conversation, became startled and stepped hurriedly into the fray.

'Holmes, we must be going, Inspector Bradstreet is expecting us on the *Matilda Briggs* case, now that this trifle has been cleared up.'

Wilde smirked at the idea of the lost pin being a trifle. 'I shall send you tickets to opening night in thanks,' he promised. Formal goodbyes were exchanged and the visitors were promptly on the street, hailing a hansom.

They did not speak of Sherlock's deductions or of the encounter with Wilde, but they sat a little apart, not even their shoulders touching, as though disaster and denunciation lurked in the air they breathed.

Back in the warmth and safety of Baker Street, John finally asked:

'I suppose it's obvious what Wilde and Lord Alfred got up to at the theatre last night, but how did you know?'

Sherlock scowled. 'The signs were all there. I've no doubt the pin came loose during the... the embraces that led to the unsettling of the shelf. One or other stood on the brooch and the chalk. They tidied to cover their tracks, but carelessly, and went on to complete their tryst elsewhere in the theatre. I didn't look for signs of it. I could hardly bring it to the manager's attention. If I do not shine a spotlight on the evidence, the theatre can deny all knowledge of it.'

With that, Sherlock snatched up his violin and stalked about the parlour making a dreadful racket. John eyed him briefly then made a point of examining his moustache in the mirror on the mantel.

'Perhaps Wilde is right,' he said aloud. 'I could shave it. If it doesn't suit me I suppose it will grow back.'

The violin fell silent. 'I forbid you to listen to that wastrel. Oscar Wilde will end badly. The man has no discretion and overestimates his own cleverness, and London will allow men like us to survive only so long as we remain hidden.'

John turned to Sherlock. 'No. He isn't as clever as he thinks. He's not even half as clever as you, my dear. Nor a quarter as handsome. But how did he know about us?'

Sherlock's shoulder twitched in a shrug. 'He doesn't. Or he was only guessing. Probing for a response with his comments on...' Sherlock's lips twisted in a snarl. 'The Hellenic Ideal.'

John walked to him and placed a hand on Sherlock's wrist. 'Which you attain already, my dearest.' He raised Sherlock's fingers to his lips and kissed them. 'Don't be jealous.'

'Don't be ridiculous,' Sherlock denied hotly.

'It would be a rare and brave new world, if we could stroll not arm in arm but hand in hand in Regent's Park,' John said gently. 'If women, and the occasional dandy, would cease to regard me as a lonely widower and know I was already in someone's care. But I pay as little attention to the women seeking husbands as I do to somewhat over-feted Irish writers. My heart is pledged, even if I wear no ring to prove it.'

And in an instant, Sherlock was himself again, calm and settled. He took John's hands in his and regarded the bare finger on which John once wore his wedding ring. He had removed it after his official mourning period for Mary was over.

'He will come to a bad end,' Sherlock repeated. 'Beauty and poetry will not protect him from distrust and disgust if he fails to be discreet.'

'Then we will not make his mistakes,' said John. 'To begin with, you're much more clever than he is.'

Sherlock's mouth quirked in a smile. 'I don't think I will go to see his play. Wilde is certainly no embodiment of *An Ideal Husband* and, well...' His warm smile promised a continuation of their morning's interrupted activities and implied the completion of that sentence: *and you are.*

# God Rest Ye Merry, Gentlemen

DECEMBER 24<sup>th</sup>, 1894 was not Holmes' and Watson's first Christmas together, except for the many ways in which it was.

They had of course celebrated the season many times since that first year. 1881. A friendship begun through necessity in a cold January was forged, through strange adventures, into trust and devotion that ran deeper than either would confess to. In those years of friendship and buried love, a season celebrating joy was always a touch bittersweet. Then came the years of loss, when Holmes had abandoned the married Watson to his wife, and Watson thought his Holmes dead.

Their first Christmas together as lovers was spent on the *Eastwind*, heading home from Australia to England. The dangerous final confrontation with Moran was still ahead of them then. That Christmas Eve, a frisson of uncertainty persisted over whether their new-declared passion would flourish or wither in crowded London: in the return to a life imbued with their old habits of not daring to love.

A year on, Moran was no more and they dared, oh, *how they dared* to love. Discreetly, perhaps, but deeply. Devotedly. They had their home, their sanctuary, and a trusted friend in Mrs Hudson.

'Open it,' John urged that second Christmas Eve, handing Holmes a parcel wrapped in brown paper and festive ribbons. John sat on the upstairs bed in nothing but his nightshirt and a devilish smile. His moustache was in disarray from kissing his darling, who sat beside him in linen drawers and his mouse-brown dressing-gown, bare-chested, bare-footed.

Sherlock's lips were voluptuously pink from kissing. He tolerated the interruption to their languorous love-making with good humour.

'You never have the patience to wait for Christmas Day,' Sherlock said fondly, turning the parcel over and over in his nimble fingers. He breathed in the scent of the rectangular package. 'A tin of my favourite thinking tobacco from Bradleys,' he announced with a smile, 'but it is heavier than my usual supply. You've hidden something inside it.'

John's smile gave no clues, though his eyes were soft with sentiment, and his left thumb was tucked under his palm to rub at the underside of his wedding ring.

*Oh. That ring.* John hadn't told Sherlock about it; only worn it and waited for Sherlock to notice. To *deduce.* The noticing had taken seconds. The deducing a little longer, as Sherlock put out his hand for the item and John duly placed it in his palm.

The band looked almost exactly like John's old wedding ring, only the gold shone bright with its new-minted gleam. On examination, Sherlock observed an incredibly fine thread, visible on the inside curve. White horsehair from one of his own violin bows, he surmised. A new ring fashioned to look like the old. A symbol of John's marriage and widower-hood turned into the secret symbol of another love altogether.

Sherlock had solemnly placed the ring back on John's finger. In the privacy of their home, he kissed John's fingers.

'Not too mawkish for you, then?' John had asked.

'It is both camouflage and clue,' Sherlock responded, eyes sparkling, 'and thus perfect.'

Another in a long line of consummations had followed that evening.

Now, Sherlock's fingers ran over the wrapping. *This is about the ring. But it is not a ring of my own. I could hardly wear a wedding band without exciting comment.*

'You can try to deduce it from now until Boxing Day,' laughed John, 'or open it.'

Sherlock pulled the ribbon free; unfolded the brown paper; opened the tin of strong shag tobacco from Bradley's, and looked at the red velvet pouch within. He plucked it out, putting the tin aside, and shook the pouch's contents into his hand.

A heavy gold sovereign fell into his palm. In appearance it was very like an English sovereign, but Sherlock's keen eyesight caught the *M* etched below the imprint of St George slaying the dragon and above it, the date – 1893.

Sherlock held the Melbourne-minted sovereign up between thumb and forefinger to examine it better. The gesture also hid his expression for a moment.

'For your watch chain. If... if you would do me the honour.'

Then Sherlock remembered again (and how wonderful to remember it time and again this year) that he didn't have to hide that expression any more, when they were alone. He tucked the coin into the palm of his hand and met John's gaze, warmth for warmth.

'The honour is mine.'

John's proud, happy smile was another gift to hold onto. He leaned towards Sherlock and they kissed.

'John,' Sherlock murmured against his mouth, 'I have something for you too.'

He disentangled himself from the embrace, placed the coin on the bedside table, and clambered off the bed to fetch a paper-wrapped parcel from under it. 'Merry Christmas, John.'

'You hid it under my bed?'

'This afternoon while you were listening to the carollers committing atrocities against *O Holy Night*.'

Like Sherlock before him, John examined the wrapped gift. The shape of it was unmistakeable. 'A new walking stick,' he said, hefting the length of it in his hands. At Sherlock's sardonic eyebrow, he only grinned before tearing away the paper.

The shaft of the walking stick was of dark red wood surmounted by an unusual bulb of darker wood, marked all over with natural hollows and polished to smoothness.

'The body is made of redgum,' Sherlock began, 'the handpiece...'

'Banksia,' John finished for him, running his fingers over the stick. Australian woods; a superbly crafted and handsome piece. 'Sherlock, it's beautiful.'

'I thought it fitting,' said Sherlock, sitting back on the bed.

John's grin grew wicked, then – an expression much and often encouraged by Sherlock Holmes.

John ran the polished banksia bulb of the stick against Sherlock's cheek, then under his jaw, and held Sherlock in place this way while he rose to his knees and kissed Sherlock soundly. John stroked the hilt of the stick down Sherlock's throat, over sternum and belly, over the top of the linen drawers.

'How should I thank you for this splendid gift?'

'Any way you like.' The nonchalance of Sherlock's tone was at odds with the flush of his cheeks, the brightness of his eyes, and the spread of his knees.

'Off with these, I think,' said John.

Sherlock obliged, hastily shedding drawers and robe. John traced the line of Sherlock's thigh muscles with the stick.

*Gracilis*, Sherlock named the muscles, seeking some measure of control instead of gasping his helpless desire at every touch, *Adductor Longus. Rectus Femoris*, ah, d-dorsal vein, f-f-frenulum...

Then stick was replaced by busy mouth (*moustache, oh yes, good*) and Sherlock's fingers curled into the cloth of John's nightshirt. He tugged at the linen. 'Off with this. Off!' John happily and speedily obeyed the command.

Later, spent, they subsided to contented calm, Sherlock's head on John's chest. John kissed his hair.

'Wake me before you leave?'

'We'll wake together,' said Sherlock. 'The weather is miserable and it's Christmas. There'll be no clients to rouse us in the morning. Our apartment doors are locked and I've told Mrs Hudson that we'll light the fires ourselves tomorrow. We're safe.' This luxury, of waking together without fear of discovery, was another gift Sherlock had arranged for them both.

John brushed his fingers across Sherlock's jaw, the gold of the wedding band gleaming in the moonlight from the window.

*I will fix the sovereign to my watch chain in the morning*, Sherlock decided.

'Merry Christmas, my darling.'

'Merry Christmas, my dear John. My dearest boy.'

A kiss sealed their murmured Yuletide salutations.

The year ahead would bring their challenges – Black Peter, Jonas Oldacre and Colonel Valentine among them. But this Christmas Eve held the secret of their strength and success. Sherlock Holmes and John Watson were united, indivisible and steadfast.

A wedding band, a golden sovereign, and a walking stick made of native woods from the land where they rediscovered one another declared it so.

# Winter Ice

JOHN WATSON HAD MISSED many things about Sherlock Holmes during the bleak years he thought his dear friend (his dear love) was dead, but Sherlock's annual lament of how winter crushed the inventiveness out of the criminal classes wasn't usually among them.

Now, with it just over a year since Sherlock had been restored to 221b Baker Street, John would have preferred to be listening to the complaints in front of a blazing fire than skulking by the Thames, wondering which of them might freeze death before their quarry made an appearance.

At home they could have been smoking contemplative pipes in companionable silence. Sherlock could have warmed the sitting room with an air on the violin. They might have taken the opportunity to press their slippered feet together, or even steal a kiss if they could be sure Mrs Hudson wouldn't intrude.

But of all London's criminals, one had dared the most bitterly cold February in a decade to commit a robbery and a murder and have the temerity to imagine he could get away with it.

'Don't write this case up, John,' said Sherlock, his breath fogging almost before it passed his lips as they waited in the killing cold.

'Assuming we survive the morning, certainly not,' responded John, teeth chattering.

'It's hardly been a test of my powers of observation,' added Sherlock.

John, who felt it had become a severe test of his patience, particularly now that tiny icicles were forming on his moustache, declined to say anything reassuring.

The matter in Fenchurch Street had been puzzling to begin with. Cloth merchant, Miles Bollen, had been found dead on his parlour floor, his horribly wide-open mouth full of blood-tinged water, his clenched hand holding a grey-brown stone. Several indoor plants in the parlour had been carefully upended, the soil left in neat piles on the carpets and floorboards. The small mounds bore traces of fingers having raked through the detritus in search of something. The decorations had also been neatly stripped from a small Christmas tree, likewise tipped over, and left in a pile.

Within a half hour of the discovery, Bradstreet called Sherlock in to review the peculiar crime scene. Bradstreet insisted that the man could not possibly have drowned inside his own home, far from any source of water, yet was severely annoyed when Sherlock Holmes agreed with him in the most ironic manner.

'You cannot have it both ways, Bradstreet,' Sherlock admonished him. 'He either drowned or he did not; and he did not.'

'He can't have,' growled the Detective Inspector in aggrieved accord. 'But his mouth was full of water.'

'His mouth, but not his lungs, isn't that right, Doctor Watson?'

John, with his by now considerable experience with an infinite variety of sudden death, replied, 'The lack of froth around the mouth and nose suggest water inhalation has not played a part in the poor fellow's death. An autopsy should confirm it. His lips are blue and his eyes bloodshot, however, which suggests he suffocated. The appearance of blood in the water is peculiar, though. If only I had some light.' The sun was up, somewhere behind thick clouds, but inside the house it was darker even than the streets.

Sherlock obligingly held his lamp as close as he could and John peered into the dead man's open mouth. 'There appears to be a wound at the back of his throat.'

'Smooth or jagged?' Sherlock asked swiftly.

John peered closer. 'It presents as an uneven hole rather than a cut, as you'd get from a blade. A pointed weapon, something blunter than a screwdriver, I would think, though with a thickened or rounded tip. I wouldn't have thought the wound was deep enough to have caused his death.'

'What do you make of this chip missing from the front tooth?'

'I'm no dentist, Holmes. It might be recent or years old.'

'Check again at the back of the mouth, Doctor.'

John, always ready to follow any clue thrown to him, inspected the wound. He straightened. 'The medical examiner will have to confirm it, but yes, it looks like the missing portion of tooth has fallen onto the back of the throat.'

'Ha!'

'You've solved it?'

'Not yet, but I know how he was killed.'

In answer to the looks of inquiry, Sherlock threw open the unlatched shutters, allowing the drift of cold air to transform into a freezing blast. He leaned out of the window at a precarious angle, face turned up to the eaves. 'Ah, it's as I suspected. Do you notice the stalactites of ice here?'

'There's a gap,' Bradstreet observed.

'Our killer seized his moment. See these marks on the sill and in the snow by the wall? The shutters are not unlatched by chance, either – see here?'

Bradstreet inspected the window frame where the latch had been jimmied to allow the sash to be raised, and further furrows and splinters where the same instrument had been wriggled in between the shutters to deftly raise the hook from its matching eye latch.

'Yes, yes,' he muttered grumpily, 'we did see how the miscreant got in and out, Holmes. We're not actually lost without you. He came in this way, ransacked the parlour and was discovered by the unfortunate Mr Bollen before he could make his escape.'

'I imagine he was discovered while in the act of departing,' Sherlock replied, ignoring the inspector's gruff mood. 'When confronted, the intruder opportunistically snapped off a hanging icicle to use as a weapon.'

'And a struggle ensued,' said Bradstreet firmly.

'Not much of one,' Sherlock blithely contradicted him. 'There are few marks on the carpet except at the window. The plants have been upturned in a neat and methodical sequence, the search undertaken swiftly but not in a panic. No chairs or other furniture have been particularly disturbed, but see on the carpet here, mud and slush, and clear signs that two men fought briefly. During their tussle, the intruder grasped for the icicle, turned and stabbed it with some force through Mr Bollen's mouth, piercing the back of his throat and knocking him to the ground, perhaps dazing him or knocking him out cold. The conical shape of the icicle broke one of the victim's teeth and closed his airways. He didn't drown, as we concur. The killer abandoned him to his fate. Poor Bollen, who must surely have been unconscious or addled, or he would have removed the ice blocking his throat, suffocated on the blockage. After which, the icicle melted and filled his mouth with water and blood from the wound. The fragment of broken tooth was not swallowed but settled at the back of his mouth as he died.'

'That's gruesome, Mr Holmes.'

'It is, Inspector.'

'And did the killer find what they were after?'

Sherlock held the stone that had been found in Bollen's hand between forefinger and thumb. 'I imagine he found more of these.'

'That pebble?'

'That rough, uncut diamond,' Sherlock corrected him. 'Almost certainly from Monday's robbery of Ralph Parlowe.'

Sherlock referred to the assault two days ago of a young fortune hunter, attacked and left for dead within hours of his return to London from South Africa. Witnesses noted that Parlowe had dropped a pouch of pebbles, the contents spilling onto the street. The assailant, concealed with hat and scarf, had gathered up the pebbles and run into the night. Parlowe was still in hospital, barely conscious, as yet unable to speak.

Bradstreet cursed. 'That explains Parlowe's fate,' he said. 'A fortune in rough diamonds.'

'So this Mr Bollen is the man who nearly killed Parlowe?' suggested John.

Bradstreet grudgingly agreed. 'Must be. The neighbour says Bollen returned from a cotton-buying trip on Monday – I suppose he met Parlowe on the ship and he recognised those stones or the lad let it slip.'

'Then who killed Bollen?' asked John.

Once Sherlock had determined the murder weapon had been an icicle, the heart of the whole matter unravelled to his genius. Bollen's murder had not been pre-meditated but the killer's panicked assault and departure after so careful an examination of the room were, he said, suggestive.

Suggestive of what, he wouldn't readily divulge.

'As you say, Bradstreet, you are not lost without me. I wouldn't want to muddy your own investigation with my...' he flicked his fingers in delicate dismissal, pretending to be the dilettante that some of the Yard thought him. '...passing fancies.'

Bradstreet was annoyed enough to let him get away with it. 'Indeed not, Holmes, and the maid has already spoken to us of a friend of her master's, one Mr De Luca, an Italian jeweller from Vauxhall. Bollen was a cloth merchant and would hardly know what to do with a handful of rough diamonds. I've no doubt he meant to go in partnership with De Luca, only the Italian got greedy.'

'You may be right. Watson, we'll leave the *professionals* to their work.'

'This isn't the way home,' observed John.

'Indeed it is not.'

'Where are we going then?'

'To London Bridge Hospital, to see how young Mr Parlowe is faring.'

John shuddered and tried to withdraw into his coat, scarf and hat like a turtle. 'Kind of you, I'm sure, but it's rather cold for social calls.'

'My poor, dear fellow.' Sherlock hooked his hand through John's elbow and encouraged a brisker pace. 'I know your old wounds give you the devil in winter, but I may have need of you.'

As always, when Sherlock had need of him, John stood taller and walked faster, ready for any challenge.

'However I may be of service to you, Sherlock.'

'Good man. Though it may be your medical skills rather than your martial ones I call upon.'

'I'm sure Parlowe is getting the best care available.'

Sherlock only smiled.

When no cabs could be hailed on the eerily quiet streets, they walked briskly on in the feeble morning light through the snow and slush. They crossed London Bridge, aware of the Thames shifting sluggishly below, its murky waters cluttered with floes of filthy ice that scraped and squealed uncannily where they collided.

A few minutes later they were arguing with the nurses at London Bridge Hospital, demanding access to their gravely ill patient. While Dr Watson was presenting his credentials, Sherlock slipped past him, down a hall and into Parlowe's room. He returned a moment later.

'Has someone's coat gone missing?' he asked. 'Also a hat and scarf? Gloves, perhaps?'

The matron look startled before resuming her expression of severe and implacable non-co-operation. 'That is none of your business, sir, and I would thank you to leave us to our patients!'

Sherlock appeared cowed by her towering indignation.

'The nurse is quite right, Watson. We're disturbing the peace of these good people at an unreasonable hour of the morning. We shall return later.'

John was irritated until he saw the look of satisfaction on Sherlock' face, tempered with some concern, as they left.

'What are you up to, Sherlock?'

'You saw how the matron reacted. The absence of the garments has been noted.'

'What does it mean?'

'It means I did not allow for the effect of the weather on Mr Parlowe's injuries. He is not yet returned.'

'Returned?'

'His room was empty, John, and his bed quite cold. But the staff will raise a ruckus if we tell them so, and that will alert Parlowe if he's trying to sneak back in to his room. It's best we wait outside.'

Which was how they came to be loitering by the Thames in the freezing cold, when John would much rather have been at home, and for preference still in bed, trading lazy kisses with his darling. If his darling could be persuaded that it was good use of a winter-blighted Wednesday morning.

John shuddered convulsively, head to toe. He had never been so cold in his life. His boyhood in Australia and service in India and Afghanistan had not prepared him for this freakish weather in the slightest. Those countries had instead offered the opposite problem – oppressive and scorching heat. But he had loved the sun. His 1893 journey to Australia, and return a year ago with Sherlock at his side, had reminded him how much.

The memory only made the cold seep further into his bones and he made a low noise of impatience. Sherlock was keeping too much of his own council while he huddled here, hands, feet, nose and arse freezing to the accompaniment of ice floes grinding together in the Thames.

Icicles on his moustache might be the least of his worries, soon. He knew through his locum work that hundreds were succumbing to hyperthermia, this brutal winter. He might be one of them if Sherlock didn't get them out of the cold soon.

A moment later, John felt the pressure of Sherlock leaning against him. 'John, here...' Sherlock took him by the lapels of his coat and turned him, so that their bodies were pressed close, and Sherlock's breath was warm on his face.

'Ah. My poor John. You love London as I do, even when London does not love you back. You are suffering badly in this cold.'

'And-d-d y-you're not-t-t?'

'I have the constitution and frame of mind to endure in all seasons,' he said smoothly, then, in a spirit of comradery, added, 'I will confess, though, that I am not comfortable.'

John huffed a laugh that turned into chattering teeth. Sherlock rubbed his gloved hands briskly down John's arms.

'This is foolish of me,' Sherlock declared, sotto voce. 'You should return to the hospital. I'll bring my quarry in when he shows his face.'

'Absolut-t-tely not!' John declared, louder than Sherlock would have wished, but Sherlock only chastised him with a look of mild concern.

Then they heard muffled, uneven footsteps and the soft curses of someone in pain.

A man was limping slowly off the bridge down to the embankment, making unsteadily for the hospital, grasping onto the wall on one side for balance as he shuffled along. Undoubtedly Mr Parlowe, he was swathed in a coat too large for his narrow frame and a hat too large for his head, with a scarf wound tightly around his face and throat between the two.

Sherlock's solicitous manner towards John fell away and he became as bristlingly bright-eyed and focused as a hound with the fox in sight.

Unfortunately, the fox saw the stranger ahead of him perking up and took immediately evasive action. He turned quickly, only to slide perilously on the slippery path. In trying to run, his feet disappeared from under him and he fell. Then he tried to scrabble away as Sherlock, with John in his wake, loomed closer.

'No!' cried John, alarmed, as Parlowe slithered over the path, down the incline and into the swollen river. For a moment it seemed he would dash into the icy waters in an attempt to rescue the flailing man, but Sherlock yanked him back by the scruff of his coat.

'No! You'll freeze to death with him!'

Sherlock blew hard on a police whistle he drew from his pocket, then cast about for some other way to assist Parlowe.

He leapt at a row of empty skiffs, stuck in ice and mud on the riverbank, retrieved a boat hook and attempted to hook Parlowe and bring him ashore. Parlowe had lost the hat and was now sinking under the weight of his waterlogged clothes. His skin was turning blue.

'Come on, man,' Sherlock admonished him. 'Try to grab it!'

Shouts indicated someone had come to Sherlock's whistle, and a moment later Bradstreet and a constable had joined them on the path. Between the three of them, they managed to hook Parlowe by the coat and drag him ashore, his sodden, stolen coat rimed in frost.

Despite John's attempts at aid by the river, and further attempts to revive him inside London Hospital where they brought him, Mr Parlowe could not be made to breathe again. Instead, those who had tried to save him were posted in front of the fire and fed hot tea and beef broth, with hot bricks at their feet, while Sherlock laid out his reasoning for all to see.

'I thought it unlikely that the thief and killer would be a close friend of Mr Bollen's – this De Luca could have as easily been shown into the parlour by a maid and had plenty of time for a search. The fact of the intruder coming in through a window suggested he knew he would not be welcome at the door.'

'How did Parlowe even know his diamonds were in the Bollen's parlour, hidden in plain sight, as it were.'

'He could hardly have known that in advance,' Sherlock corrected Bradstreet calmly. 'Parlowe knew Bollen from their time on the ship from South Africa. Perhaps Bollen had even invited the lad to call, before he discovered what a fortune he held and succumbed to the temptation to take it by force. No, Parlowe came to retrieve his stolen goods and, expecting to be turned from the door, chose to force an entry. He was lucky that Bollen had thought to conceal what looked like ordinary stones in his plants in the very room he first entered. And of course, extraordinarily unlucky to have been discovered just as he had recovered the gems and was about to leave.'

'But how was he able to get to Fenchurch Street in the first place? He was gravely ill.'

'It is a simple matter to pretend to be more gravely ill than one is. I've done it myself. The trick is to not let competent medical staff get close enough to discover the deception.' Sherlock's gaze slid quickly away from John's at this statement. 'The staff at London Bridge Hospital are, like all London's hospitals, vastly overworked with the numbers falling prey to the cold. Parlowe only needed to exaggerate his poor health – neither speaking nor moving – until he had a moment to get away.'

'But why didn't he report that he knew who had attacked him on Monday?' John asked.

Bradstreet had to sheepishly report that he'd had a summons to the hospital from Mr Parlowe but had lacked the time to follow up. 'We are short on staff and it's difficult to get about,' he said gruffly, then refused to comment on Sherlock's raised eyebrow which clearly said, *well, we managed it.*

'He must have worried that Bollen would dispose of the diamonds before the police could be called in,' said John, 'and took matters into his own hands, after first stealing a warm coat and accoutrements for the journey.'

'Exactly, Watson,' said Sherlock warmly. 'I have no doubt that Signor De Luca was to have cooperated with Bollen to cut and sell the diamonds. But Parlowe recovered them first, only to be confronted by the man who had betrayed his friendship and nearly killed him.'

'So he seized on the first weapon he could find – an icicle – and killed his enemy,' observed Bradstreet.

'His aim was either perfect or macabrely lucky, but he did the deed and fled. But once in the cold again,' Sherlock continued, 'the weakness of his wounds slowed him considerably, particularly after his murderous exertions. If we attempt to follow his path from Fenchurch Street, I expect we'll find he stopped at a public house or coffee house to shore up his strength before making his way back here. Thus we were able to beat him back to his hospital bed.'

Bradstreet took a pipe from his pocket and lit it, prompting a longing look from the two men beside him. 'It is a shame the lad is dead; he might have escaped a hanging, with that story.'

'It's a sorry one, certainly.'

'How did you come to be so close at hand when Holmes blew the whistle, Inspector?' John asked after a moment. Sherlock smiled to himself but forbore to comment on how long it had taken him to ask.

'De Luca hadn't left his house since Sunday, on account of him being abed with ague – his wife and staff all accounted for him there. Someone sat with him round the clock, fearing he was at death's door. I thought it best to come to the source, that is, Mr Parlowe, as Mr Holmes had already done, as the only other man who knew about the diamonds. It was good timing, or bad, depending.'

Sherlock's eyes sparkled and Bradstreet scowled.

'What will happen to the diamonds, sir?' asked the constable, who was also recovering from the cold.

'Whatever's in Parlowe's will, I suppose. His mother will likely inherit. Cold comfort that it is.'

The constable sighed and dragged his attention back to his cooling tea. 'I wish this had some brandy in it,' he muttered.

John wholeheartedly wished the same.

After their tissues and circulation had been restored, John and Sherlock were able to summon a hansom to take them as far as the nearest underground station, which took them to the Baker Street stop, from whence they could walk back to their lodgings.

And then they were at their own door. Mrs Hudson fussed while they hung wet things in the hall, and bustled up after them to stoke the fire and make sure they had blankets for laps, more hot bricks for their feet and warm brandy to sip.

At last she withdrew, however, and Sherlock seized the moment to sit on John's lap, clasp John's hands in his own and briskly rub them for warmth. He left those ministrations to take up kissing, which also heated both of them quite well.

'There, my dear John, blooming to life again. Winter is hard on you at the best of times.' He referred to the aches in John's shoulder and leg.

'I am quite content now, my darling,' John replied languidly.

'I can tell.' Sherlock's grin was wicked.

John's cheeks flushed pink, but his eyes were bright with anticipation.

Blessedly, Mrs Hudson let them be for a good long while, which they spent in Sherlock's room, reviving one another expertly after a very trying morning.

'Soon enough it will be spring,' Sherlock assured him afterwards, lazily kissing John's fingers as they lay under the blankets, 'and I will take you to the park to watch the buds. You'll be warm in London again.'

'It is spring every day since your return,' John said, capturing Sherlock's jaw and kissing his mouth.

And they warmed each other through again, in their haven from the snow.

# The Case of the Vinegar Valentine

DR JOHN WATSON RETURNED to Baker Street, damp of clothing, mood and spirit, after responding to an urgent summons from a demanding patient. He left the bone-chilling mid-February fog at the door and trudged upstairs to find Sherlock Holmes still at breakfast and studying an item from the first post. Only partially dressed, in trousers and shirt but lacking collar, coat and shoes, Sherlock was draped in his dressing gown. John would have found Sherlock's deshabille more charming if he hadn't been so sorely in need of hot tea.

'Was your early patient worth the cab fare?' Sherlock asked, not looking up from the envelope.

'He paid well, if that's what you mean,' grumbled John, hanging his fog-dewed coat on a peg with his hat and thick scarf.

'Not well enough for eight in the morning,' Sherlock noted.

'It was hardly the declared emergency,' agreed John, toeing off his shoes before jamming his numb feet into his house slippers. 'Mr Rose's condition was indicative of indigestion, lack of exercise and an overactive imagination. I've suggested he hire a live-in nurse, if he just wants to waste good money being fussed over. Someone better suited to taking his temperature, holding his hand and telling him he's good for another thirty years yet.' He stood in front of the fire now, palms to the flames, close enough to the heat that steam curled faintly from the hems of his trousers.

'Well, and so he should,' said Sherlock firmly. 'You're claimed already.'

NARRELLE M. HARRIS

John turned to Sherlock to see a flash of a grin and his grey eyes sparkling, and his sour mood lifted at once.

'A happy Valentine's Day to you, my dear,' he said in a hushed voice, even though no-one but Sherlock was around to hear.

'And to you, John. Come, sit down,' urged Sherlock. 'I've kept some breakfast warm for you.'

John obeyed, squeezing Sherlock's shoulder fondly before sitting opposite. He helped himself to tea, still hot enough thanks to an ugly but efficient beadwork tea cosy. Sherlock pushed a covered plate towards him, one of several on the table, which turned out to be kedgeree.

John tucked in with the appetite of a man who'd spent a cold February morning in a distant house at a ridiculous hour, tending to a needy hypochondriac. He washed down the first mouthful of curried rice and fish with tea and, while piling up his fork again, asked, 'What has caught your attention so thoroughly? A new case?'

'Perhaps,' Sherlock conceded. He passed the envelope he'd been studying across the table.

John examined it while despatching another mouthful. Addressed to Sherlock, the broken seal on the flap and the unmistakable quality of the cream paper suggested a sender of considerable wealth and social standing, though no name was appended.

'Sent from Piccadilly early this morning,' John noted. 'A man's handwriting. Educated and bold, though the letters are ill-formed towards the end. Perhaps he's elderly, or suffering from an injury or some degenerative disease. Drink's always an option.'

'Scintillating, my dear Watson!'

'Am I right?'

'You'll have my report at the conclusion,' Sherlock declared, amused. John warmed a little more under that smile. Sherlock had his own methods of rewarding John for a puzzle well deduced, several of them employing his fine and expressive hands. 'If you have nothing more to share about the envelope, it's time to examine its contents.'

Sherlock folded back the flap and eased two items from the fold: a letter on the same luxurious paper and several pieces of waste paper and card wrapped in a blank sheet of fine tissue paper.

The memory of rewards for correct deductions past, and with his immediate hunger assuaged, John examined each of them in turn.

The watermark of an unknown crest in the thick cream-coloured writing paper confirmed the writer's likely prosperity. The very brief letter said simply:

*Mr Sherlock Holmes,*

*Lord Sterling Quincy will call on you this morning at 11 o'clock to discuss the meaning of the enclosed, and what may be done about it, whatever your fee, for I do not believe a word of it.*

*Sent in expectation of swift resolution.*

The signature was full of dramatic, self-important swirls and underscores.

'The gentleman seems to be in some agitation,' John said. 'He writes so furiously that the nib has punctured the paper in several places – quite a feat given its thickness.'

He had thoroughly warmed to their game. Within his profession, John was an investigator too, studying the individual for indications of current symptoms, as well as exploring medical history, home circumstances and recent changes to gain insight into his patients' condition. His deductions were specialist and focused on medicine, however, and his capacity to deduce about the wider world required too much generalist knowledge. So far, he was following Sherlock's own path of reasoning about this Lord Sterling Quincy – but soon he would get no further, and Sherlock would make the next leap for him.

'And?' Sherlock prompted

'Lord Sterling Quincy – I don't know the name, but the superior tenor of his letter is hardly surprising for a man of his rank.

High-handedness seems to come with the title, for some of them. But see how he abandons formality for 'I do not believe a word of it'. He is, as I say, deeply agitated.'

'Could you say why?'

'I imagine the answer lies here.' John folded back the tissue paper wrapping to reveal the torn pieces of a hand-made card. The item had been sundered with some violence. The delicate paper lace was in shreds, though, as John reconstructed the card like a shabby jigsaw puzzle, its charming presence was deeply at odds with the bizarre hand-drawn image in the centre of the card.

The drawing, though monstrous, was skilfully rendered. A young and fashionably dressed woman was grotesquely saddled and bound in a bridle, which the maker had created in brown ribbon. Her expression was one of anguish. The decoupage around her, of hearts and roses, made her bondage all the more jarring.

'I'm not surprised our client tore it up. Though, as Valentine cards go,' John mused, 'it's not the strangest I've seen.'

Sherlock, who had given John one of the cards in question, only prompted him to turn it over.

John obeyed, to find a poem printed in neat blue ink and precise lettering.

*Good sir, I am not yours to possess*
*To groom and breed like your horses.*
*You may not dictate whom I see*
*Or when my kin may visit me.*
*Do not believe I will be idle*
*While you trap me with a bridle.*
*Your arrogance and peacock pride*
*Warn me not to be your bride.*
*'Gainst your conceit I have revolted*
*And you will find this mare has bolted.*

'Ah,' said John with dawning understanding. 'I see.'

'You do?'

'One of those acid Valentines I've read about,' said John. 'They're an unkind thing to send to an unwanted suitor, though I suppose they do the trick. Unless it's meant as a joke?'

Sherlock arched an eyebrow.

'Not a joke,' John agreed. 'The doggerel is very specific, particularly with that outrageous cartoon on the front. I'm not surprised this Lord Sterling is very agitated.'

'That is your conclusion?'

'Perhaps his Lordship wants us to discover who sent such a brutal Valentine's greeting,' he suggested as he checked the time on his pocket watch. John knew perfectly well he'd fallen short of a real conclusion, but he wanted another cup of tea and a buttered roll with cold sausage before they had to prepare for their visitor at 11.

Sherlock tutted but without real censure. 'We have time, but don't let me keep you from your breakfast any further...'

John had half a buttered roll in his mouth already, and waved the knife encouragingly for Sherlock to elucidate.

'Lord Sterling is not an alcoholic, although he's a man with clear demands on his time,' Sherlock said, flapping the envelope in his left hand. 'He addressed his missive after he had already completed the letter, and rage was getting the better of him again. You raise an eyebrow. Yes – *again*. As you pointed out, he has written with such force that the ink could hardly leave the pen quickly enough to keep up with his words – see how evenly it is disbursed in the address, which he took care to inscribe without error, and how thin it is throughout this very short message. The gentleman was impatient and beyond merely agitated, as the tears in the paper showed you. This is no joke and he knows the sender: he states he 'does not believe it' and has hastened the letter and card to us ahead of his arrival. This is not a man with time to waste. Given his anger and urgency, one wonders what took precedence over his coming directly to Baker Street.'

John dabbed crumbs from his moustache. 'I don't wonder he's angry. That poem accuses him of very unchivalrous behaviour. Though her judgement may be sound,' he continued, musing. 'I've met one or two few lords falling short of that chivalric ideal.'

'Ah, my John, it's a minor miracle that you are not more jaded.' Sherlock pressed his hand over John's, a fleeting fondness before he rose, a second before a sharp rap on the door signalled their client had arrived.

Lord Sterling Quincy was as impatient and agitated as his letter had signalled; and full of the pride and arrogance of which the poet had accused him. He whipped past Mrs Hudson as she tried to announce him, gave the breakfast dishes a coldly disapproving frown, dismissed John's presence with barely a glance, and tilted his chin at Sherlock as though commanding a response to his puzzle this very instant.

Sherlock did not invite Quincy to take a seat. Instead, he looked past him to thank Mrs Hudson for bringing food and fresh tea up for Dr Watson – 'He was sorely in need of refreshment after that emergency death-bed summons!' (John had to bite his inner lip to keep from scoffing at such a technically accurate yet completely misleading description.)

As Sherlock turned back, Quincy, without waiting, snapped, 'Well?'

'Lord Sterling, I can hardly begin to find your fiancée on an hour's notice when I know nothing beyond her penmanship and a certain wit for rhyming couplets. Save your fury,' he added, when the lord became flushed with indignation. 'Give me facts. How did you receive this card – by mail or was it hand delivered?'

Quincy's rising temper was checked only by Sherlock's imperturbable coolness. He drew on his fine breeding and met the detective with equal hauteur.

'Miss Davenport's letter was delivered by her father's footman to my butler, who gave it to me. On reading it, I went to her home to confront her and discovered she had vanished. I despatched my letter to you immediately.'

'But you didn't come to me at once. Why not?'

'Sir Ellis Davenport had a notion his daughter may have gone to stay with her aunt. He asked that I not act until he'd received a telegram from Reading. The aunt's negative reply arrived just before I set out for this appointment.'

'You have wasted valuable time in not coming to me at once, and more in not including the envelope in which the letter came,' Sherlock admonished him thoroughly. 'Do you still have it? No? Do you remember any distinguishing marks on it? Was it addressed or did it come simply you're your name, or was it blank? Was it addressed in your fiancée's handwriting or another's? In what mood was the footman when he delivered it – do you think he knew the contents? Really, I do not see how I can proceed with so little data.'

Quincy's face was a portrait of constrained rage. Yet he swallowed his pride and in a strained voice said, 'As I am in need of your services, I shall overlook your impertinence.'

Sherlock, uncowed, waved his lordship aside, to his lordship's obvious wrath, and John thought for a moment he would have to intervene, perhaps with the poker. He was moving surreptitiously towards it when Sherlock clapped his hands together and continued.

'Well, I shall have to make do. What else can you tell me? You state in your letter,' he said, leaving his client in no doubt how inadequate he thought the letter to be, 'that you do not believe Miss Davenport sent this card to you of her own free will. But you acknowledge that it is in her handwriting?'

'It is very like her hand, yes. But Matilda is a very dependable girl and sensible of the honour of what becoming Lady Sterling Quincy will mean to her and her family. Mr Holmes, she must be found and returned to me at once.'

Sherlock sobered and nodded, suddenly seeming to be aware of Quincy's importance. 'You have a picture of the lady?'

Quincy, prepared at least this far, handed Holmes a photograph; a stiffly posed engagement portrait. Lord Sterling Quincy stood behind the seated Matilda Davenport. She was a handsome, elegantly dressed young woman in her twenties. Her bearing was regal yet good-humoured and her gaze to the camera was bright and intelligent. Quincy's expression was much more formal and his hand on her shoulder was not light – the material beneath his fingers was slightly ruched with the firmness of his grip.

'Very well. I shall take the matter in hand,' Sherlock said, tucking the picture into his pocketbook. 'I have hopes I shall be able to bring you news this afternoon. Will you be at home? It is best that you are,' he went on without pause, 'I may need to obtain further details from you and would like to obtain them without delay. I shall let Mrs Hudson see you out. Dr Watson! I'm sorry to drag you out into the winter air again, so soon after your mercy dash, but there must be no delay! Here are your gloves, your hat and scarf, come!'

John found himself bundled out of Baker Street at monstrous speed and was only saved from slipping on the icy footpath by virtue of Sherlock's steadying hand on his elbow.

'What the devil...?' John demanded.

'Miss Davenport is in some danger, of her liberty if not of her life,' Sherlock said as he finished winding his scarf around his throat.

'You know where she is?' John asked, astonished.

'Not yet, but I have suspicions.'

'On so little evidence?'

'On a good deal of evidence, and from the lady's own hand.'

Their first call was to Rotten Row, prompted by the equine nature of the card. Though few riders were out in the cold, the excursion provided several instructional conversations from locals who worked nearby, even at this frosty time of year.

'Oh, I know her, right enough,' an ostler, Jack Stowe, said on sight of the picture. 'Marvellous with 'er horses, I remember specially. Hisself with her, he's not bad but he's a bit free with the whip and hard on the bit, which is hard on the horses. She more coaxes 'em. 'Spose it's horses brought 'em together. The Davenports breed racers. I've won a bob or two on 'em. Rumour is, his Lordship's not doing so well. Had to sell half his stable, I heard. Racing's a rich hobby for rich folks.' Stowe pretended serious concern, but underneath it thrummed the glee of a man who felt a member of the quality had it coming.

The woman wrapped in winter woollens and tending a pan of roasting chestnuts had things to add. Sherlock's questions to her were more oblique. He folded the portrait to show only Miss Davenport.

'She's not in trouble, I hope,' Molly Betts said. 'She was here only the other day.'

'Riding?'

Molly laughed. 'She was! And in this weather! She came to me after, for chestnuts, and that brute Quincy, pardon me, *Lord Sterling*, gave her such a telling off.'

'He raised his voice to her?'

'Not a gent like that, but he spoke all hissing-like, like she was a naughty child and not a rider twice as good as him. She's been riding here for years, but oh, no, he don't like her riding the Row without him. He don't like her hair or her hat or her clothes or her cousin what she rode with.'

'What did the lady say?'

'Nothing. She's a proper lady. But ooh, if looks could slap he'd have had a palm print to wear home on his cheek!'

'Vividly put,' John noted as they went next to the Davenport's home in St John's Wood. 'Our client seems consistently unpleasant.'

'Our client,' Sherlock responded crisply, 'is not his lordship.'

At St John's Wood, they called on Matilda Davenport's worried father. Informed that they had been engaged to find her, he readily sent Matilda's maid, Annie, into the parlour to speak with the detective.

Annie was stoic about the notion that her mistress might have been abducted; smirked slightly at the suggestion she might in fact have run away. Sherlock also managed to exchange a few words with the footman, James, who insisted he hadn't known what the envelope contained, only that his mistress had asked him to deliver it in person.

Taking their leave, Sherlock examined the stairs and the short drive, and asked James a pointed question.

'A carriage was here this morning,' said Sherlock. 'It departed before the household was up. Do you know anything about that?'

'Nothing, sir,' replied James very rapidly. 'All our carriages are where they ought to be, sir. You could count 'em. Sir.' His tone was defensive and, John would have said, not entirely truthful.

'Quite,' said Sherlock approvingly. 'Good lad.'

Sherlock hailed them a hansom to Victoria Station.

'It's a long shot, John,' he said, 'but perhaps the odds are shorter than I fear.'

John, long used to Sherlock's close-lipped ways on cases, had been listening carefully to the various conversations.

'You think she's eloped with another?'

'I wouldn't go so far, but I'll very much surprised if she isn't at the station for a boat train to the continent.'

'But she hasn't any luggage!'

Sherlock arched an eyebrow at him. 'We ourselves once took to the continent with nothing but a carpet bag each.'

A dark memory to be brought up, but it brought another to John's recollection. 'Nelly Bly! She went on her infamous trip around the world in 80 days on short notice, and had no more luggage than we did. It was commented on as unusual, at the time, that a woman could travel with so little luggage.'

'Miss Davenport's card contained a good deal of vinegar,' Sherlock said approvingly. 'I'm sure that the young lady possesses considerable spirit. Certainly more than will be constrained by that bully of a man.'

'Why are we going to find her, then? Surely we won't fetch her back to him.'

'Oh no,' Sherlock agreed, before occupying most of the drive with scribbling a list of European addresses on the back of the photograph.

Through fortunate timing, they found Miss Matilda Davenport just as she was waiting to board the boat train, just as Sherlock had surmised. She wore a handsome travelling dress of good quality and a large, brand new carpet bag was at her feet. She drew herself up on seeing them making their way towards her on the platform, chin up and eyes blazing.

'If you've come from that awful man, I may as well tell you you'll be wasting your breath! I wouldn't marry him if he promised me a kingdom.'

John hid his surprise at the slight flatness in her vowels. She spoke well but all the elocution lessons in the world could not hide the origins of her accent. For a short time as a boy, living with his father and brother on the goldfields of Ballarat, he'd also picked up the flat, nasal twang of Australia. John and his father had departed in such a hurry, and in such disgrace, that John had soon scraped the sound of that accent out of his tongue. Not even Sherlock had ever detected even a hint of it. He gave no direct sign of hearing it now, but John knew Sherlock too well to think he'd missed it in Miss Davenport.

'Though it's true he engaged me to find you,' Sherlock reassured her, 'we mean nothing of the kind. My name is Sherlock Holmes...'

Her eyes widened. 'I've read about you. So you,' she said, looking to John, 'must be Doctor Watson. Sterling came to you? I never imagined he would. It seems so against his nature.'

'Indeed,' agreed Sherlock. 'The fact that he did is why I have so many qualms about your fate should he find you. He seems a man of uncertain temper at the best of times, and that card you sent him has made him angry.'

Her eyes opened wide with her incredulity. 'He showed you the card?'

'He tore it into pieces, but realising I would need a spur to take on his case, he delivered the fragments to Baker Street.'

'I shouldn't have sent it,' she confessed, 'but I wanted to be certain he would leave me alone this time.'

'Unfortunately, for a man of his temperament, your rejection has had the opposite effect. I'm of the opinion that he aims to search until he finds you. I'm sure he will pursue a way to coerce you to the altar. Possibly with your father's aid.'

Miss Davenport's expression ran through a cascade of expressions: distress, grief and shame, but also irritation and defiance.

'That may be the case,' she said fiercely. 'I've tried three times to end the engagement, but my father pleads Sterling's case every time, and ensures the ring I've returned comes back to me. I promised to give Sterling another chance twice before, but now I'm decided. Nothing will induce me to marry him.'

Sherlock Holmes read volumes in every line of her face, her dress, the carpet bag in lieu of other luggage, her accent, her readiness to set out unchaperoned, her truculent Valentine's Day card and her fearlessness in the face of two strangers.

'Let me put your mind to rest, Miss Davenport,' said Sherlock, with that earnest, intelligent warmth that so often led people to trust him. 'Doctor Watson and I mean first to be sure of your safety.' Before she could protest he continued, 'And we now have that assurance. Since you depart so rapidly on your journey, alone and with little luggage, it is clear to me you are a woman of independent means. An extended stay on the continent is well within your means.'

Miss Davenport found this amusing, her mouth twisting in sardonic good humour. 'I am so glad that my arrangements have met with your approval.'

Not to be put off by her lack of appreciation for his form of chivalry, Sherlock went on to become less delicate. 'Be frank with me, Miss Davenport. Since this clearly was no love match – I take it this was an arrangement more of convenience?'

She failed to take offence, having now decided that this interference was droll. 'It was the convenience of a fortune in exchange for a title. Our family's wealth comes from mining in Victoria and in property in Sydney. I have my portion from my late mother, with no need for me to live off my father's income if I had a mind to my own investments. To be fair as possible to Sterling, we seemed a good match at the start, with our shared interests in horses. But he bullies his horses, he bullies his staff and he bullies my father, who is too impressed with Sterling's title to stand up to him. He attempted to bully me, too. I told him I wouldn't have it, and Sterling stated outright that no wife of his would ever defy him. So I decided to be no wife of his. He has his pride, but so do I.' Her lifted chin and glittering eyes were back. 'So what is your plan, Mr Holmes, now that you've found me.'

'My only intention,' said Sherlock, 'is to offer some advice. More than Quincy's pride has been hurt. My cursory investigations so far suggest he's a long way up queer street, likely with gambling debts. He won't give up your dowry easily. '

Matilda Davenport laughed. 'Well, he'll have to accept defeat. I'm not staying to argue the point. I'm off to Spain to learn more about Andalusian horses. I'll write to my father to tell him that I'm safe, of course, and my maid Annie will join me there soon.'

'I strongly advise that not even your father should know where you're staying, if he is as swayed by Quincy as you say.'

'You think Sterling that dangerous to me?'

'I do,' said Sherlock. 'I expect him to be following in my footsteps very shortly, in fact – I sent him home to wait for news but I doubt that will hold him long. He's already been searching for you, and only came to me when he could make no progress. He'll be on the hunt again soon.'

'What do you suggest?'

'Travel straight on to some other destination and telegram me at Baker Street when you can. We will send Annie to a hotel we know in Dover to await your instructions. Then take a Grand Tour; travel as much as you like. I have taken the liberty of writing a list of recommended hostelries in Germany, Austria, Switzerland, Portugal and Spain. Doctor Watson and I once went on our own Grand Tour, and you'll be received properly at them all, for as long as is required.'

'Annie and I won't have to stay away forever, surely?'

'Not forever. I have some other plans to enact. Write to Baker Street regularly and when I have news I will send it.'

'Really, Mr Holmes – this is terribly irregular.' Matilda Davenport only pretended to be scandalised. Her bright eyes gave away her amusement. 'It sounds like a wonderful adventure, so I'll do as you say.'

'Excellent. Ah, here, your train is departing soon. You'd best board and be away, Miss Davenport. I'll be in touch.'

John had been mostly silent during this entire exchange and for the walk to the street to flag a cab. Inside the hansom, rattling towards their new destination, he frowned.

'You recommended the Englischer Hof at Meiringen.'

'It is a very good hotel.'

'It...' John's cheek twitched.

Within the safety of the hansom, Sherlock pressed his hand briefly over John's. 'The Englischer Hof is not to blame for the events that took me away from you.'

John knew that. The blame for Sherlock's departure and long absence lie directly with the two of them, and the unresolved feelings that had made their lives increasingly untenable. All resolved now, but sometimes the old wounds of the heart returned.

'I wish...' John began, but he'd wished so much, so often, without effect, that he gave up the phrase again now. He could wish as much as he liked that he and Sherlock had taken a different path, earlier on, but that would have been against their natures and their knowledge at the time. He sighed. 'But you're back in London, now. Home. With me.'

'Yes,' said Sherlock. He squeezed John's hand and they sat in more companionable silence until they reached Quincy's house in Mayfair. Quincy himself was just leaving the large but slightly shabby house, striding towards a waiting carriage.

'Ah, my Lord!' Sherlock called to him, alighting rapidly from the hansom before it had completely stilled. 'You're ready to be on the move! Excellent! If you hurry, you may intercept the lady at her destination!'

'Holmes!' protested John.

Quincy tilted his chin up. 'Spit it out, man!'

'Miss Davenport was quite genuine when she sent you her card. She has broken off the engagement,' said Sherlock.

'We'll see about that,' growled Quincy. 'I won't be humiliated like this. I'll fetch her back at once.'

'It's a little late for that,' Sherlock said apologetically. 'We traced her footsteps to a train to Southampton this morning – which, as you know, is where ships depart for ports in Australia. A contact in the shipping office telegrammed to confirm she boarded the *Coromandel* for Sydney, which weighed anchor this afternoon.'

'She's sailing for Australia?'

'I'm afraid so. Perhaps it is best to wash your hands of her.'

A man of more normal temperament might have accepted that his fiancée no longer wanted a bar of him and given up, but Quincy's prideful rage, not to mention his apparently desperate need for a ready fortune, would have none of it. He barked orders for his valet to pack a trunk and to send it on after him.

'She'll learn I won't be trifled with,' Quincy muttered, and was off to book passage to Sydney in the wake of his absconding fiancée.

That evening, Sherlock and John were warming themselves by the fire, having dined on an excellent fowl. Now they sat companionably, smoking pipes, their slippered feet slightly touching. They drew their legs back briefly when Mrs Hudson brought up two late telegrams and left her tenants to themselves again, possibly to spend an evening indoors with her own particular friend.

'Ha!' declared Sherlock. 'Confirmation from my friend Moss in Southampton. The *Eliza Clare* set sail yesterday, with Lord Sterling Quincy on board in a second class cabin. Miss Davenport will have several weeks' grace while he pursues his promised fortune across the sea with all the fervour of a hound after a fox. And this is from the fox,' he said, waving the second telegram. 'Our resourceful client has set off for Lisbon, where we are to send the faithful Annie. Miss Davenport has told her father she means to study art in Paris, which is the one city she will avoid.'

'You say 'our client'...' John said, eyebrow arched, with a smile as sardonic as that of the young woman in question.

Sherlock placed both telegrams on the fire. 'In spirit if not in fact,' he said. They both contemplated that with some satisfaction.

After a moment, John reached into the pocket of his smoking jacket and withdrew an envelope. He handed it to Sherlock and leaned back again, choosing to look into the fire rather than at Sherlock.

'John...'

'It is the 14$^{th}$ today,' John said. 'I promise it's not as tart as Miss Davenport's, and not as sentimental as your expression suggests you fear it will be.'

Sherlock slit the envelope open with his thumbnail and regarded the contents – a plain blue card on which was drawn an Australian gum leaf; beneath it, written in elegant cursive, *Always* – with studied neutrality.

Sherlock's neutrality was hard tested. He sighed slightly. Traced the word with his fingertips. 'Always, John,' he promised in return.

'You'll have to burn it, too,' said John, a touch sadly.

'Let me memorise it first.'

'All right.' John's smile bloomed.

And their slippered feet touched again, while they sat in harmony, treasuring their Valentine.

# Bored

*(This story is in the form of a 221B – precisely 221 words long, with the last word beginning with B)*

In the privacy of Baker Street, John brushed a farewell kiss against Sherlock's cheek. Sherlock delighted in the details: a soft lower lip; the sweep of neat moustache; warm breath scented with tooth powder; John's happy hum.

Then John withdrew hum, breath, bristles, lips, to don his scarf and hat.

'Ask Mrs Hudson to keep some supper hot for me?' he said, retrieving his gloves. 'It's a bitter day and I'll want warming when I return.'

Sherlock forbore from mentioning other ways John might be warmed. He simply waved languidly as though John's departure were nothing to him (fooling nobody).

'Update your commonplace books,' suggested John.

Sherlock rolled his eyes in perfectly dramatic ennui. 'All this great city has left for me to do is *filing*. While you take your *useful* and *necessary* skills to London's *indisposed*.'

'I promise to send for you if I discover a poisoning.'

Sherlock's shrug anticipated no such luck.

'Chin up, my dear,' said John. 'Someone's bound to use this fog to devise villainy worthy of your skills.'

'True.' Sherlock brightened, then drooped again. 'Until then: *tedium*.'

John tugged gloves over his capable, clever hands; traced a leather-clad finger down Sherlock's jaw.

'Not,' he said, 'if you apply your imagination to how you'll welcome me home.'

A fine challenge, inspiring wicked grins: Sherlock's imagination was boundless.

# The Beekeepers Children

THE EMPTINESS ALONGSIDE John Watson as he woke had the quality of bad dreams: *not right* and yet *accepted*.

A marginally more wakeful thought then occurred to John: *he'll be in the kitchen or out with the bees.*

At last, memory caught up with consciousness, and John's next thought was once again and always, *Please, God, keep Sherlock safe.*

John lay lonely in their bed, still suspended between *not right* and *accepted*, while the rest of his daily litany unspooled in his thoughts.

*Is Sherlock's mission over? Is he on a ship home yet? Is he in London, debriefing with Mycroft? He is coming home to me, surely, if all has gone to plan. Unless, God, dear God, he is d...*

Through the bedroom wall, in Sherlock's former study, John heard a frightened, wailing cry and then another voice, a soothing murmur. The pain in both moved him, but he was selfishly grateful for their disruption too. It kept him from following the awful direction of his own thoughts.

'Shush now, Davy. Shush.'

'I can hear the bombs, Bobby.' Davy's voice was a fragile sob.

'It's just a bad dream, Davy. See? Here we are in Sussex, safe and sound.' Bobby Wiggins' tone was softly encouraging, sunny and kind as always.

Davy's panicked panting breaths quietened.

*Poor lads,* John thought, glad again he had been able to offer them a billet – two narrow beds in place of Sherlock's desk and cabinets and laboratory equipment. Those things were packed away Sherlock's upstairs bedroom now, rarely used even when Sherlock was at home. Neither of the men next door could have managed the stairs.

(John often sat upstairs now, holding Sherlock's pipe or his magnifying glass, or clutching his coat and breathing in the fading scent, aware that he was trying to wish Sherlock home by force of will.)

Bobby spoke again, sadly this time. 'Won't you look at me, at least?'

Soon after, John heard Bobby's halting steps to the doorway of the billet, and down to the bathroom. Minutes later came the heavy clump of Davy MacKee's foot and the scrape of his crutches; the clatter of the crutches tangling with a chair. The creak of Davy sitting back down on the bed. The sound of the young man weeping.

With a sigh, John swung his feet out of bed, reached for his cane and prepared for another day of waiting with the bees.


'Tea for you, Doc.'

The cup clattered onto the table, sloshing tea, but John only nodded thanks. Bobby eased himself onto the seat opposite and reached for a slice of bread and the honeypot. He found spreading the honey awkward and switched the knife to his more flexible but non-dominant left hand. He screwed his mouth into a determined pout and made the best job of it he could.

'It'll get better,' said John quietly.

'Me or him?'

'Both of you.'

'Not the eye, though.' Bobby bit into his breakfast, chewed, and met John's gaze with defiant cheer.

One of the young man's eyes was as bright and clear as ever. The other was murky within the scarred socket, and saw only shadows now.

'No, not the eye,' John replied, 'but your coordination will improve.'

Bobby flexed the fingers of his right hand, likewise scarred. The damage all down the right side was awkward, but no longer painful.

'Reckon it will,' agreed Bobby, 'I'm not a looker like before, but then, my brother Will says I didn't have many looks to lose.' He grinned, irrepressible even in the face of injury. He was like his father, Bill, that way.

'Well, looks aren't everything. I've managed perfectly well without them all my life.'

Bobby laughed out loud. 'You're too modest, Doc Watson. There's some consider you right handsome, I bet.'

'I doubt it.' *And the only man who would agree with you is not here to defend me against myself.* But John smiled. Sherlock would only have berated him about false modesty in any case. 'Still willing to help me with the bees again today?'

'Why not? Can't see they can do worse to me than the Boche, eh?'

'Holmes insists that treated correctly, bees are better company than most people.'

'Yeah, but most people, treated correctly, as he says, are all right too.'

John and Bobby wore bulky white beekeeping suits into the meadow, too cautious to emulate Sherlock's bare-handed inspections. Bobby wore Sherlock's own rarely-used suit and smoke scented veil. He walked without Sherlock's grace, especially with the way his now-healed injuries truncated his movement, but his slowness seemed to suit the bees.

They carefully smoked the bees calm and checked the progress of the hive. To keep Sherlock's records up-to-date, John noted the colours of the pollen, from which Sherlock would know where the bees had foraged, and checked the queen's laying pattern to make sure it was even.

Bobby was conscientious about brushing bees away from the box edges while John replaced the inner cover and lid. The boy's care made John think of Sherlock, which made his heart clench and his eyes prickle, so he made a joke.

'I knew I would get on well with the bees when I discovered we have something in common.'

'You're both uncommonly fond of Mr Holmes?' offered Bobby with a wealth of affection.

John was more surprised by Bobby's unaffected warmth than his knowledge, but he huffed amusement. 'Two things in common, I suppose, then. The bees and I all find tranquillity in a good smoke.'

Bobby was kind enough to laugh. 'Now I see all those little bees puffing on tiny pipes,' said the lad, 'and looking around with wee magnifying glasses to pronounce on the habits and histories of the flowers!'

John laughed too, but the heart-hurt closed his throat suddenly.

Bobby's gloved hand patted John's white-shrouded shoulder. 'He'll be home soon, Doctor Watson, right as rain, you know what he's like. And he always comes home to you.'

John mastered himself. 'Well, there are times when I have to go and fetch him,' he said.

Sherlock spent the weeks before he left England training John how to look after the bees and keep the records on their behaviour, marking up books and leaving him notes. John still found notes randomly, in cupboards, in books, tucked into the pockets of his coats or the heels of his boots.

Some of the notes didn't strictly relate to the bees.

*Some bees forage very far from the nest in search of necessary pollen, yet the bee will return to the hive and its Queen. Always.*

John wasn't as easy with the bees as Sherlock, but he took his commission seriously. He used his best bedside manner with them, speaking encouragingly, kindly and gently to them, making no sudden movements. John was clever enough to learn quickly, brave enough to not be cowed by the threat of stings, and sentimental enough to be soothed by the tasks of beekeeping. He felt that by taking care of them, he was caring for Sherlock, too.

He thought the bees knew he, and now Bobby, weren't Sherlock. It gave him a feeling of solidarity with the hive, to feel that the bees missed Sherlock. He became superstitious, though. He felt he mustn't let anything happen to the colony; these bees that Sherlock had raised. If anything happened to them, it would be a harbinger of Sherlock's fate.

Sherlock would have scoffed at the notion. John knew it was ridiculous. Illogical, unreasonable, even damaging, to think of them that way. It didn't stop the thought, or keep him from tending them as perfectly as he knew how.

Davy MacKee was at the kitchen table, fixing the clock, when John and Bobby returned from the meadow. Davy's crutches rested at an angle against the wall. The stump of his left leg swung in time with the tock of the timepiece as he tested the mechanism.

'Post's come,' he said, pointing with the delicate screwdriver but not looking up. 'Tea's brewing.' The pot sat on the end of the table, steaming fragrantly, the cups arranged about it, along with the jar of last harvest's honey. Davy's shirt was more rumpled under one arm and his hand was reddened where he'd had to grip the crutch tight in the effort to manoeuvre cups and pot to the table over numerous trips. John didn't comment on it. Davy wouldn't thank him for noticing the effort it had taken to do something so normal.

Bobby poured tea while John took up the letters addressed to Dr J.H. Watson. He put aside the ones addressed to S. Holmes; pleas for help with strange puzzles, most of them. *The Strand Magazine* readers didn't know Sherlock was away applying his gifts to a larger good.

Davy glanced up at Bobby. 'There's a letter from your Ma,' he said. His gaze fixed briefly on Bobby's ruined eye then returned to the clock.

Bobby sighed and opened the envelope.

'Ma says she's heard from Will,' he said with brittle cheerfulness. 'He's coming home on leave, all in one piece too, which is a relief. Don't know as Doc Watson has got room for another recuperating soldier, though the bee shed's warm enough to doss in at a pinch. At least it's dry and nobody's shelling it.'

At the table, Davy MacKee finished screwing the back of the clock into place. 'I don't reckon the bees'd take to William like Dr Watson says they've taken to you. He's all fidgety.'

Bobby grinned. 'He's got ants in his pants, Ma says. And anyway, I'm sure the two of us is enough to be getting on with, eh Doc?'

'I'm very glad to have you both here,' said John. It had been lonely in Sherlock's absence, until Bill Wiggins wrote to ask if Dr Watson knew where his Bobby and Bobby's friend Davy could get out of the noise of London to recover their nerves. The quiet here did both boys good. Not enough good yet, mind. Some things, as John knew to his chagrin, could take years to sort out, if the men involved were fools enough.

He had no notion how to remedy that, however, so he leafed through his correspondence. The first letter was from Stamford, the next a missive from the British Medical Association. The third...

John abandoned his tea and tucked the third letter into his coat pocket.

'Hand me the wool and needle, Bobby,' John heard Davy say as he headed for his room. 'Might as well make myself useful with some darning.'

81

John sat on the side of his bed, put on his reading glasses, then slipped his thumb under the flap of the envelope, tore it carefully open and shook out its contents.

The grubby slip of paper bore a sketch in fine black ink, of John Watson's own eyes, rendered perfectly, down to every line of his 64 years – minus the ones he'd developed since Sherlock had been summoned to a mission for His Majesty.

Fingers trembling, John lifted the paper and inhaled its scent. It smelled of soot and ink. He couldn't discern anything of Sherlock's scent on it: but he had touched this paper. Within the last week, Sherlock had drawn this image, sent it with his dispatches to Mycroft to forward onto John. He had sent the only message he could.

*I live,* said the message, and *I remember you in every detail; you are always with me.*

It said other things too.

John brushed his fingers over the ink. He folded the paper in two again, to protect the drawing, pressed the back of it reverently to his lips, then set it onto the bedside table. He opened the top drawer and withdrew his old cigarette case: that once heartbreaking memento that Sherlock had left for him on a mountainside in Switzerland.

The cigarette case contained precious things – the letter Sherlock had written to him, believing he was to die at Moriarty's hand. An 1893 telegram summoning John to Australia, which had caused so much anger and led to so much joy. Now it also contained the series of Sherlock's sketches, the only communication he could safely make to John, keeping his patient vigil in their Sussex cottage.

John took the drawings out. He had nearly wept ten weeks ago on receiving the first confirmation that Sherlock was at least recently well – a carnation etched in faint green ink – and then laughed. Green carnations, indeed.

The second, a month later, was a delicate rendering of a willow tree. *Their* willow tree, its sheltering branches sweeping over the creek, where springs and summers and even warm autumn days, they stretched out together, to talk, to kiss, to give and enjoy pleasure.

Two weeks ago, John had added a simple sketch of the Southern Cross constellation, under which they had first declared their love and first consummated it.

John placed the new drawing with the others into the cigarette case, and placed the case back into the drawer. It was no good sitting here pining. There was work to be done.

John sat by the front door to pull off his muddy Wellington boots. Beside him was a basket of beans, marrows, a few tomatoes, from their garden. He'd enjoyed the last hour there, weeding, pruning and picking ripe produce for their dinner. He had worked surrounded by the scent of the soil and the hum of the bees, thinking about the day Sherlock had knelt beside him in the garden and found a golden Roman coin in the dirt. Sherlock had kissed his cheek. 'Ah, my Boswell, always at hand for the great discoveries!'

Now, as he tugged at the boots, John thought he might go upstairs and look for the coin. He'd meant to drill a hole in it for Sherlock to wear on his watch chain.

A voice rose, anguished, from beyond the door that stood ajar.

'Why won't you look at me, Davy? Do I horrify you that much?'

John listened. (A terrible habit, this eavesdropping, developed over years of working with Sherlock Holmes. He shouldn't listen. Or he should make a noise. But he listened.)

'Don't, Bobby. Please.' Gruff. Terse.

'It's not so bad, you know,' said Bobby, the cheerfulness a thin, cracking veneer over pain. 'It still works a little, and the other's as fit as a fiddle.'

'Don't, Bobby.'

'Look at me, Davy. Please. Don't take on, so. Open your eyes, now. Unless you just can't bear to look at me anymore.'

'And what of me?' Davy's stricken voice was a match for a broken spirit. 'How can you bear to look at *me*? I don't want to see how you'll look at me, Bobby. I'm a cripple.'

John remembered his own return from Afghanistan, long ago: coming home broken and full of grief, lost in spirit and mind, his nerves shattered and his health ruined. Not forever, it turned out, but when you are young and have been stripped by the battlefield, you can't know that.

'Oh, love,' Bobby said, softly, so softly, so softly and sweetly, 'I see my Davy MacKee. Even with one leg, you're still my Davy-boy. My beautiful boy. And it's awful, but it could've been worse. You might be dead, and then where would I be? How would I live? Look at me. Please, Davy. Please. I won't pity you, I promise. How could I? You saved me.'

'No. No. You saved me.' A gasping breath, tearful.

'Of course I did.' Bobby's voiced hitched in a kind of laugh. 'I'd have marched into hell to take you from the devil himself, and plugged him in the eye while I was at it for hurting you.'

John knew the story, from their old Baker Street Irregular, Bill Wiggins. At the battle of Festubert, May 1915, Private David MacKee had thrown his childhood friend clear from an exploding bomb. Private Robert Wiggins, despite the burns to the right side of his body, dragged his badly wounded friend off the battleground to aid, and refused aid himself until Davy was seen to.

Their bodies now as healed as they would ever be, these young men had found living in London too wracking to their nerves to bear, especially during the Zeppelin bombing raids. Bill Wiggins had written to John, asking for advice, and John had said, *send them to me, your son and his friend. It's quiet here, with Sherlock away for the war. I could use some friendly faces. Send the boys to me.*

John had no children of his own, but his heart hurt as a father's might for those boys, as it did for Wiggin's grief for his sons. Bobby so grievously injured, Will recently enlisted, and George, the eldest, killed in action on the Somme.

'That's it, my lad, my boy.' Bobby's choking voice was flooding again with that irrepressible good cheer. 'Look at me. See? I love you, Davy. I'd have died for you out there, and you for me, I know it...'

'I would have, Bobby.'

'And now we have to be alive for each other, and not give up.'

'It's hard, Bobby. It's *harder*.'

'That it is, my sweetheart. But we've courage enough together, don't we? I'll help you walk, and you'll help me see, and we'll get through this world side by side, like we always did.' Bobby made a self-deprecating sound, half a laugh, half grief. 'Even though my looks could curdle milk, now.'

'Shh, no, no, Bobby. You're my best boy. You're still beautiful to me. You've got a beautiful soul and there it is, right in your eyes. Yes, that one too, don't hide. If I can't hide my face, neither can you.'

Tearful breathing for a moment and then Bobby said, 'Good. Right. So you and me, Davy. Like always, like it should be. How about we show those German sons of whisky-faced eel pies we're not done for, not by a long chalk.'

A stifled giggle was his reply. 'Whisky-faced eel pies? Good God, Bobby, you can't just swear like the rest of us, can you?'

'You know my mum doesn't hold with swearing,' Bobby's tone was brighter under the mock-seriousness.

'Tell me another and make me laugh.'

'Old General Haig is a rabbit-tailed cheese wheel and a cloth-eared fathead to boot.'

Davy snort-giggled, and then their laughter turned to a promising not-silence. A rustling kind of quiet. A sighing, murmuring kind of hush.

Smiling, John pulled his Wellingtons back on, took up his cane and decided to say a long good evening to the bees.

---

John woke to that *not-right*-yet-*accepted* emptiness in their bed. He looked through his cigarette case and, like a sentimental old fool, gazed on each of the drawings. He pressed them, and the old letter and the telegram, to his cheek and pretended that each transferred the touch of Sherlock's fingers to his skin. *Soon, please God. Soon.* Then he put them all away and rose for the day's chores.

The boys were still abed. Not separate beds either, judging from the sounds during the night. John hummed Sarasate as he made tea and set out bread, butter, and condiments for the morning repast.

He went out to see to the bees, alone but gladdened. Perhaps only a touch envious. No need to open the boxes today; record-keeping was the morning's agenda. Date, time, temperature. Were the bees gathering pollen or nectar? Any sign of propolis?

In the bee shed, John found one of Sherlock's bee notes tucked under an empty jar.

*Buzz pollination is the process wherein a bee vibrates its flight muscles rapidly, causing the flowers and anthers to vibrate. This releases the pollen for the bee to gather.* Solanum lycopersicum , *for example, requires this type of pollination.*

John flushed, remembering, as Sherlock had meant him to. A warm, lazy day, and Sherlock lying between his thighs under the willow tree. Moving languidly, the scent of lavender oil, his hands on Sherlock's backside, caressing, kneading, pulling him closer. Warm breaths and murmured endearments, then languid became urgent. *Vibrating. Releasing pollen.*

'If I were a bee,' Sherlock murmured afterward, his head on John's chest, indulging in a whimsical mood, 'I should prefer your stamen to all others.'

'If I were a flower,' John had replied, his expression wreathed in merry contentment, 'I would bloom only for you.'

John folded the note to place in the cigarette case later.

A half hour later Bobby joined him, relaxed and pink-cheeked and singing 'Just a little love, a little kiss, just an hour that holds a world of bliss'. The bees hummed around him, apparently pleased by Bobby's own honey-happy song.

'If you boys want a ramble,' said John as he and Bobby made notes on the bees' comings and goings, 'there's a lovely place by the creek, under the willow tree, an easy walk even for crutches. Take a picnic lunch and make a day of it.'

Bobby, flushed and grinning, nodded. 'It's very sunny, and I noticed that willow the other day. I thought it might be nice for... picnics.' He gave John a look both sly and friendly. 'You and Mr H picnic there a lot, I reckon.'

John raised an eyebrow, mostly to cover a smirk, forgetting that the beekeeper's headgear obscured both.

'Holmes likes to swim,' deflected John.

'Me too,' said Bobby laughingly. 'A good, vigorous swim is excellent for a man.'

---

John took his cane on his walk into the village. The lane to the main road went past the disused lodge at the end of their quite large property. The cottage, this lodge, an empty stable and the bee hut that had once been a potting shed had once been part of a larger property.

John wore a rucksack to carry the bread and vinegar he meant to buy. Some string, too, he thought, and some long nails Davy said he needed to mend the shutter on the back window. Nails or screws, was it? It was on the list, either way, along with soap, tea, a bit of rabbit, if the butcher had some. A new bottle of lavender oil too, perhaps. The old bottle had mysteriously disappeared from the bathroom, and he'd begun to suspect that the bees had been so fond of Bobby this morning less for his singing prowess and more for the scent of flowers that clung to him.

A faint tang of salt was in the breeze coming in from the sea, a few miles away. Bees hummed in hedges and gardens as he walked to the village, perhaps many from their own hives. He liked to pretend they were watching out for Sherlock's return.

He was walking home, rucksack bulging with the little household items, when the county bus rattled past. He raised his cane in a salute to Mr Fanshawe, the driver, and to his surprise the bus hove to on the side of the street.

Sherlock Holmes waved to him from the bus' open door.

'Do hurry, John,' he said, affecting impatience. 'Fanshawe's running late already and we can't let his employers berate his tardiness on our account.'

John forgot his aching leg and the weight on his back and he ran, he ran, he ran to Sherlock Holmes.

They sat side by side on the bus, almost but not quite touching. John's hands were trembling. So were Sherlock's, he noticed, from the effort of not reaching for each other. Instead, John clutched the head of his cane in both hands and tried not to stare.

*He's tired. He is too thin. He's very pale. Unhurt, I think. I will examine him, when we're home. I'll touch every inch of his beautiful skin and be sure he's unhurt. I will kiss him. I'll kiss his mouth and his back and his feet. I will kiss his hands. I'll tell him he's marvellous. I'll tell him about the bees. I'll tell him how happy I am. I will tell him I love him.*

John caught a laughing look in the corner of Sherlock's eye, and grinned like a giddy fool in love, and rubbed his knuckles over his moustache to hide how foolishly happy he was.

Fanshawe pulled over at the start of the little road to their cottage, and they alighted. Only then did John realised Sherlock had no baggage but a worn leather satchel.

'Holmes, your luggage?'

The bus rattled onward as Sherlock replied, 'Everything I need is at my side.'

John beamed at him. Sherlock looped a hand through John's arm and off they walked to their cosy property, past the empty groundsman's lodge they'd not yet converted to a laboratory for Sherlock, past the meadows full of flowers and bees.

'You can't say much, I know,' said John, 'but it was a success?'

'It was, and lives have been saved. Not soon enough for George Wiggins.' Sherlock became solemn. 'I did it more for them, you know, than for King and Country. They are our Country are they not, all those boys? Wiggins' boys. Robert is here, I understand, with his young friend, recovering from their injuries?'

'Yes. Using your study as a billet, I'm afraid. Your things are all upstairs.'

'Ah.' Sherlock cast John a rueful look. The nature of the regret made warmth uncurl in John's chest and stomach and groin.

'They were at the willow tree when I started for the village,' John elaborated meaningfully.

'Ah.' Sherlock smiled this time, but not as though he were surprised. He sighed, then. 'I have sometimes wished you might have had sons and daughters, but what I saw in France and Germany, John, makes me glad we had no children to feed to that madness. It's butchery, nothing more. Worse than anything I, and I daresay even you, have ever witnessed. New weapons and new warfare have created carnage absolute.'

John placed a hand over Sherlock's on his arm and squeezed. 'Even without a war, Sherlock, I have never longed for children. Not unless they could be yours too, and with that impossibility, I have been content enough with the bees.'

Sherlock laughed. 'The bees?'

'Well, we do care for and nurture them,' said John cheerily, wanting to nudge Sherlock out of his sorrowful mood. 'It's a sentimental fancy, I suppose, but what do we do for the bees that parents don't do for their children? Except clothe and educate them, and send them out into the world to seek their fortune.' John grimaced good-humouredly at his absurd fancy.

Sherlock's cheeks dimpled in an impish grin. 'They educate us instead, and help to feed us. They go out into the world and work for the hive, and so for us. You're quite right, John, only we've missed the awkward middle years of having offspring. They support us in our dotage now, as good children ought.'

'Dotage,' John snorted. 'Ass.'

Sherlock's grey eyes crinkled. 'If our lodgers are at the willow tree, Watson, perhaps you'll be kind enough to furnish me with lunch and a thorough physical examination?'

'As your doctor and your friend, I am only too happy to oblige, my dear Holmes.'

After simple bread and cheese, eaten sparingly, Sherlock opened his mouth, like a bird, and John fed him a slice of apple. Sherlock's tongue darted out to catch a fleck of juice on his lip, and John leaned forward to kiss the residue away. They didn't speak of Sherlock's absence, or its painful echo of another, long ago.

'The bees are well,' said John, cutting another slice of apple for his love. 'They seem to like Bobby.'

'Bees don't like or dislike people, John. Though it's good to know he understands how to work with them. They certainly appeared well as we passed them by.'

John fed Sherlock, kissed him again, and said, 'Thank you for the drawings.'

'You understood the messages, then?' Sherlock caught at John's wrist and licked John's apple-sweet fingers.

John hummed assent, then his lips tilted wryly. 'Not at first.'

'But by the last?'

'*I'll see you soon.*'

'Exactly.'

'I thought the carnation was simply our little joke, though I realised by the last one you meant it to establish the meaning. Green carnation. Your secret mission, and a code for none but you and me.'

'Good. And then...?'

'The willow tree. You had identified your contacts and were in a safe place. It was a long time till the Southern Cross, but as it's used for navigation, I thought it meant you were on your way home. I hoped it did.'

'Exactly right, John.'

John kissed Sherlock's smiling mouth, simultaneously amused and touched by the pride in Sherlock's expression. 'I would be very dull indeed if I didn't work it out eventually.'

In their bed, Sherlock sprawled, all long pale limbs and wiry musculature. John, stockier, tanned from his afternoons in the garden, his golden brown hair now threads in the soft grey, knelt at his side. He had already run his sturdy hands all down Sherlock's arms and legs, over his skull and face, down his bare shoulders and back and buttocks, across his chest and stomach, satisfying himself that his Sherlock was unharmed, whole, and here, *oh here.* His eyes had been traitors to his knowledge in the past and so John needed to touch Sherlock's skin to anchor certainty in his head and heart and hands: Sherlock was *well* and he was *home*.

Sherlock smiled up at John from his pillow, and suckled on his apple-sweet fingers. Sherlock's hair was silvered now too, at chest and groin as well as scalp. Like John's, his skin was more lined than it had been, but they had no complaints. They were growing old together, after all. Those grey hairs, those lines of age, were as precious as the hearts and minds beneath them.

'My dear,' murmured John, 'my dear, my very dearest.' He kissed Sherlock's palm, his wrist, his forearm and inner elbow. 'I'm so glad you're here.'

Sherlock reached for John and pulled him to the mattress beside him, so that he could press their naked bodies close. He wound himself around John – leg over John's hip, an arm across his back – and brushed the tip of his nose against John's.

'Remind me,' he said huskily, 'of why I love your moustache.'

John's wrapped his arms around Sherlock's torso, pushed his legs between Sherlock's thighs, and tipped Sherlock onto his back on the mattress. He kissed Sherlock's cheeks and eyelids, his nose and mouth, and down his throat.

All the way down – throat, chest, belly, thighs – John kissed and nuzzled, brushing his moustache in ticklish sweeps against Sherlock's skin. Sherlock wasn't ticklish, though, and he arched happily into the sensation, pushing his cheekbones against it, and his clavicle, his nipples and navel and hips, all against the marvellous sensation of John's lips and teeth and tongue and moustache against his body.

Finally, Sherlock moaned and cursed and then laughed. 'John. Don't tease, I beg you.'

'You beg, do you?'

'As abjectly as you like, my dear, only, pl...aaahhh...' Sherlock bucked up into John's mouth as it slid over him, and sucked, hard, then soft. John released him, and Sherlock laugh-moaned again.

'You will manage what the Germans and Moriarty failed to do, and kill me dead, John Watson.'

'Never,' John swore, pressing down on Sherlock's body with the warmth and weight of his own. He kissed his love and bit gently on his lip and jaw.

Sherlock spread his knees so that John could settle more closely against him. 'Then give me satisfaction, you wicked fellow.'

John reached for the bottle of lavender oil on the bedside table.

'John, John, John, John...' was the breathless litany as John smeared oil over them. John took his sweet time to do it.

'Stop dallying,' Sherlock demanded imperiously, making John grin and use his hands and fingers to make Sherlock gasp.

'I don't dally,' John promised him, 'I do exactly what pleases you.'

'Yes.'

They clung to each other, and kissed, and thrust slow then fast then slow then fast*fastfasterfasterfaster* until their tight-wound passion unfurled in pulses, body against cherished, desired, beloved body.

John, panting, sagged against Sherlock, his face pressed into Sherlock's throat to hide his emotion. As though *that* would hide anything. Sherlock held John tightly against him and nuzzled at his hair.

'I'm home, John, and I'm not leaving you again. Not for anyone. Not for the King himself. You have me forever, now. You and the bees.'

John's laugh caught, a gasp-gulp steeped in joy. He smothered it against Sherlock's warm, perspiration- and tear-damp skin. 'Good.'

Bobby held the door open for Davy, who easily manoeuvred inside with his crutches and a pair of trout threaded onto a strip of willow around his neck

'Mr Holmes!' Bobby dashed towards the table, depositing on the floor the basket containing the remnants of the picnic. 'My God, sir, it's good to clap eyes on you. I'd have known by Doc Watson's face that you were home if I hadn't seen you for myself.'

John rubbed at his moustache, obscuring his face, but the brightness of his eyes, the jaunty angle of his head, his whole alert and satisfied demeanour were a giveaway of his feelings on the matter. Just as the fragments of grass and willow leaves in Bobby's rumpled hair and collarbone, and a tiny leaf pressed to Davy's forearm underneath his flannel shirt attested that *fishing* had not been their only activity by the creek.

Bobby seized Sherlock's hand in his and shook it vigorously, before whirling to face Davy and relieving him of the fish. 'Davy, this is Mr Sherlock Holmes!'

Davy adjusted his crutches and thrust out a hand to shake Sherlock's. 'I've heard a good deal of you, sir, and read all of Doctor Watson's tales. Welcome home, sir, it's a great honour to meet you. I've admired your great work all my life.'

Sherlock waved his hand self-deprecatingly, but his ears were pink with a pleased flush. *Still as sensitive as a beautiful girl to praise on his art*, thought John fondly.

'John says you've been very helpful about our home, Mr MacKee,' said Sherlock, indicating the clock that had not worked since Sherlock had interfered with it for an experiment, 'and that you, Robert, are very handy with the bees.'

'We've done our best, sir,' grinned Bobby, 'and Davy can fix anything he puts his mind to. Never met anyone so clever with his hands.'

Davy flushed too, now, and looked at the pot of tea to have something to look at besides everyone's knowing faces. Bobby chuckled and at last took the trout into the kitchen.

'Tea?' offered Sherlock, and Davy took a seat.

---

Supper was trout and beans from the garden with fresh bread John had bought in the village. Afterwards, there was celebratory cider.

'Thanks for having us, Doc Watson,' said Bobby, 'but I guess we'd best be going back to London. The cottage is a bit small for four...' Neither he nor Davy appeared happy at the prospect.

'It's small for the long term, perhaps,' conceded Sherlock. 'You've seen the groundsman's lodge down the lane? I planned to turn it into a workshop – John has unreasonable strictures against my using the dining table here for experiments. It never used to bother him unduly at Baker Street. In any case, the old stable behind the cottage is better placed for that work.'

'We can help clear up the stable for you, Mr Holmes.'

'That would be most kind, Bobby, but I was thinking that more of your efforts could be directed towards the lodge. It can be made cosily habitable for two easily enough. Certainly before autumn. Of course you'll stay in your billet here until then, if that's what you'd like.'

'You'd like us to...?'

'Continue to assist with us here, yes, if that suits your plans.'

'Well... if you like, Mr H. I'd be honoured. Davy?'

Davy blinked hard, as though astounded to be included in the sudden, generous offer. 'If you think I can be of service, sir.'

'You've already proven to be of service, Mr MacKee. I heard no end of it when I broke the clock and its return to working order may finally have seen me forgiven.'

Behind his cider glass, John's moustache curved up, betraying his mirthful response to that.

'Then I'd be glad to stay on, Mr Holmes.'

'Excellent.'

'A toast to the future, then,' suggested John.

---

John put on his beekeeper's suit and went out with Sherlock, attired in his hood, to look to the bees.

'They do like us, see? They recognise you, at any rate.'

The bees indeed flew close around them and crawled all over Sherlock's hands as though recognising their keeper had returned.

'It is known that bees recognise individuals. It will be part of my research to determine how. As to them liking me...'

'Why shouldn't they? I like you well enough, and I'm at least as clever as a bee.'

That set Sherlock to laughing, and the bees swirled around him as he did.

John grinned at the success of his joke. In the distance, he could hear Bobby singing, and then Davy's voice joining him as they turfed broken furniture and clouds of dust out the door of their new little home.

'So, Davy and Bobby in the lodge,' said John in satisfaction. 'That will be good for them. And for us, to have their help – and company.'

'Yes. Well.' Sherlock shrugged. 'We must leave this place to someone one day. Perhaps these two will suit. MacKee seems clever, Wiggins' boy is bright enough, and... the bees like him.'

John laughed again. Carefully, he removed one glove and placed his hand on Sherlock's wrist. In the sunny meadow, with none to see, Sherlock slipped his palm against John's.

The bees landed in a soft-buzzing cloud on their joined hands, and hummed and danced messages to each other for a long and lovely moment before flying off, in their industrious way, to make honey.

**Author's notes:** With thanks to Bobby Fries for inspiration and Britt McCombs for checking my bee facts (though any errors remain my own). The song Bobby Wiggins sings is *Just a Little Love, A Little Kiss (Un Peu D'Amour)* as sung by Maggie Teyte in 1916. English lyrics by Adrian Ross, music by Lau Silesu

# About Narrelle M. Harris

**NARRELLE M HARRIS** writes crime, horror, fantasy, erotica and romance. Her 80+ works include vampire novels, erotic spy adventures, het and queer romance, Sherlock Holmes adventures, and Holmes/ Watson romance mysteries *The Adventure of the Colonial Boy* (2016) and *A Dream to Build a Kiss On* (2018). A queer, paranormal Holmesian book focusing on Mrs Hudson as a menopausal werewolf, *The She-Wolf of Baker Street*, was released in 2024.

In 2017, her ghost/crime story "Jane" won the 'Body in the Library' prize at the Scarlet Stiletto Awards. Other works include *Grounded, Scar Tissue and Other Stories* (short-listed for the 2019 Aurealis Awards), and *Kitty and Cadaver*.

Narrelle was also commissioning editor for *The Only One in the World: A Sherlock Holmes Anthology* (2021) and *Clamour and Mischief* (short-listed in the 2022 Aurealis Awards). In 2023, she co-edited *This Fresh Hell* with Katya de Becerra. In 2024, she co-edited *Sherlock is a Girl's Name* with Atlin Merrick.

## THE SWORDMASTER'S SECRET AND OTHER STORIES

Many of Narrelle's books are published by Clan Destine Press and Improbable Press, and her work can be found on Amazon and other online retailers.

For more details, visit:

- https://narrellemharris.iwriter.com.au/
- https://www.clandestinepress.net
- https://improbablepress.com/

# Other books by Narrelle M Harris

## *The Adventure of the Colonial Boy*

1893. DR WATSON, STILL in mourning for the death of his great friend Sherlock Holmes, is now triply bereaved, with his wife Mary's death in childbirth.

Then a telegram from Melbourne, Australia intrudes into his grief. 'Come at once if convenient.' Both suspicious and desperate to believe that Holmes may not, after all, be dead, Watson goes as immediately as the sea voyage will allow.

Soon Holmes and Watson are together again, on an adventure through Bohemian Melbourne and rural Victoria, following a series of murders linked by a repulsive red leech and one of Moriarty's lieutenants. But things are not as they were. Too many words lie unsaid between the Great Detective and his biographer. Too much that they feel is a secret.

Solve the crime, forgive a friend, rediscover trust and admit to love. Surely that is not beyond that legendary duo, Sherlock Holmes and Dr John Watson in Narrelle M Harris' The Adventure of the Colonial Boy.

**Praise for *The Adventure of the Colonial Boy***
'Melancholy, sweet, triumphant, fierce in a beautiful balance.' ~ TA Creech, Amazon
'I found the second reading as exciting as the first.' ~ Heras Mom, Amazon

## *A Dream to Build a Kiss On*

John Watson, invalided army doctor and sometimes artist, and Sherlock Holmes, consulting detective, become flatmates and friends in contemporary London.

Love grows too, despite past betrayals and present dangers—for where you have Holmes and Watson, there too are Moriarty and Moran.

A Dream to Build a Kiss On, written by Narrelle M Harris and illustrated by Caroline Jennings, explores love and family, trust and betrayal, brothers and brothers-in-arms, forgiveness and revenge, in an ongoing tale told 221 words at a time.

**Praise for *A Dream to Build a Kiss On***

Exquisite in detail and structure...' ~ Angela Kam White

'A swashbuckling adventure with more twists and turns than a rabbit's warren'~ Rohase Piercy

'Caroline Jennings [illustrations]...are an absolute delight' ~ K. Caine, Goodreads

NARRELLE M. HARRIS

## *The Only One in the World*
### Edited by Narrelle M Harris

What if Sherlock Holmes was Polish? What if he or John Watson were Indian or Irish or Australian or Japanese? How would their worlds look if one or both was from a completely different background?

In *The Only One in the World,* we asked a baker's dozen of writers to answer these questions, and the marvellous results are adventures in Ancient Egypt, Viking Iceland, and 17th century England; in 19th century Ireland, Germany, and Poland; in South Africa of the 1970s and New Orleans of the 1920s; and in contemporary Australia, USA, Russia, India and Portugal.

**Praise for *The Only One in the World:***

"In many ways these are tales about the human condition...even though their ostensible focus may be a crime and its detection" ~ Arts Hub

"Smart, entertaining, and fresh" ~ The Weekend Australian

"The stories are exciting and fresh, breathing new life into a beloved character" ~ Ashleigh Meikle

"Cool...cool...cool' and 'Cool!" ~ Phil Brown, Courier Mail

## The She-Wolf of Baker Street

After Sherlock Holmes 'rescues' Audrey Hudson from a kidnapper, she offers him her upstairs flat in exchange for solving the unsolved murder of her family in Edinburgh. Sherlock's being forced to theorise without data, however – he doesn't know his new landlady and her late family are werewolves. There's a lot he doesn't know about his attractive new flatmate, John Watson, too.

Momentum is added to the case as Sherlock's investigations suggest a much bigger mystery is at play, involving a disturbing case on Dartmoor with a Greek interpreter; Sherlock's agoraphobic sister, Myca; Audrey's long-dead love, Ruby Stockton; and the fate of Great Britain's mystic heart.

Will Holmes be able to unravel the mysteries that have haunted Audrey's life? And can Audrey protect her new pack, or is she about to lose those she loves once again to unknown enemies?

**Praise for** *The She-Wolf of Baker Street*
'Brilliantly executed' ~ Ashleigh Meikle
'A touching and unexpected view of 221B Baker Street through werewolf Mrs Hudson's familiar yet brand new eyes' ~ Wendy C Fries

# Sherlock is a Girl's Name
## Edited by Narrelle M. Harris and Atlin Merrick

What would the Great Detective be like if Sherlock Holmes was a woman?

That's the question answered in Sherlock is a Girls' Name, an anthology imagining Sherlock Holmes as female, in tall tales that follow the great detective across time and even space.

The stories in this collection, selected by long-time Sherlockian editors Narrelle M. Harris and Atlin Merrick, imagine Holmes in deep space, 1990s Russia, Victorian London, contemporary USA, worlds of magic and more.

Holmes' many Watsons include ghosts, robots, a young boy who doesn't speak, a teenage tuba player, a stranger on a plane – and that's just to start. In each story Holmes and her Watson do what they do best: solve crimes and have adventures!

Anthology authors include: Tansy Rayner Roberts, Eugen Bacon, Sarah Tollok, Verity Burns, Dannye Chase, Kenzie Lappin, JD Cadmon, Stacy Lawhorne, Karen J. Carlisle, Katya de Becerra, Millie Billingsworth, Narrelle M. Harris, and Atlin Merrick.

**Praise for Sherlock is a Girl's Name**

"This collection is a delight. Make some tea, snuggle in, and go on a journey with Sherlock Holmes" ~ Sarah Tollok

"I loved reading the stories in this collection so much – I just want to wrap them up in a hug!" ~ Jennifer Bradshaw

"I really enjoyed this book. In fact my only complaint is that one of my favorite stories is too short!" ~ ReneCat

"An entirely fun collection" ~ Julie

# Don't miss out!

Visit the website below and you can sign up to receive emails whenever Narrelle M. Harris publishes a new book. There's no charge and no obligation.

https://books2read.com/r/B-A-RKTUB-BJTSD

**BOOKS 2 READ**

Connecting independent readers to independent writers.